Neq was young and inexperienced
both as a lover and as a warrior. His
skill in the circle developed quickly,
until no man could beat him – at
least not fairly. But this was a skill
which he was going to need, for Neq
was the chosen one – the warrior
upon whom rested the future of the
Empire, and whose own future lay
entangled with that of an ill-fated
woman and the ruins of a dream . . .

Also by Piers Anthony

SOS THE ROPE
VAR THE STICK

and published by Corgi Books

Piers Anthony

Neq the Sword

CORGI BOOKS
A DIVISION OF TRANSWORLD PUBLISHERS LTD

NEQ THE SWORD

A CORGI BOOK 0 552 09824 8

First publication in Great Britain 1975

PRINTING HISTORY
Corgi edition published 1975

Corgi Books are published by
Transworld Publishers Ltd.,
Cavendish House, 57–59 Uxbridge Road,
Ealing, London W.5.

Made and printed in Great Britain by
Cox & Wyman Ltd., London, Reading and Fakenham

Neq the Sword

CHAPTER ONE

"But you are too young for the circle!" Nemi Cried.

"If I am, then you are too young for that bracelet you've been eying! You're fourteen—the same as me." His name was the same as hers, too, for she was his twin sister. He refused to use that name now, for he no longer considered himself to be a child.

In fact he had already chosen his manhood name: Neq. Neq the sword—as soon as he proved himself in the battle circle.

Nemi bit her lip, making it artfully red. She was full-bodied but small, like him, and could not term herself adult until she had borrowed the bracelet of a warrior for at least a night. After that she would shed her childhood name and assume the feminine form of the warrior she indulged. Between bracelets she would be nameless —but a woman. And twice a woman when she bore a baby.

"Bet I make it before you do!" she said. But then she smiled.

He tugged one of her brown braids until she made a musical trill of protest. He let go and walked to the circle where two warriors were practicing: a sticker and a staffer. It was a friendly match for a trivial point. But the metal weapons flashed in the sunlight and the beat of the weapons' contacts sounded across the welkin.

This was what he lived for. Honor in the circle! He had

taken a sword from the rack in a crazy hostel four years ago, though it was so heavy he could hardly swing it, and had practiced diligently since. His father, Nem the Sword, had been pleased to train him, and it was excellent training, but he had never been allowed in a real circle.

Today he was fourteen! He and his sister were no longer bound by parental conventions, according to the code of the nomads. He could fight; she could borrow a bracelet. Whenever either was ready.

The sticker scored on the staffer, momentarily stunning him, and the two stepped out of the circle. "I'm hot today!" the sticker cried. "Gonna put my band on someone. That girlchild, maybe—Nem's kid."

They hadn't noticed Neq. His sister's challenge, "Bet I make it before you do," meant nothing. But though they were close as only twins could be, their rivalry was also strong. Neq had a pretext to act.

"Before you put your band on Nem's girlchild," he said loudly, startling both men, "suppose you put your stick on Nem's boychild. If you can."

The sticker smiled to cover his embarrassment. "Don't tempt me, junior. I wouldn't want to hurt a nameless child."

Neq drew his sword and stepped into the circle. The weapon looked large on him, because of his small stature. "Go ahead. Hurt a child."

"And have to answer to Nem? Kid, your dad's a good man in the circle. I don't want to owe him for roughing up his baby. Wait till you're of age."

"I'm of age today. I stand on my own recognisance."

That silenced the sticker, because he wasn't familiar with the word. "You *aren't* of age," the staffer said, looking down at him. "Anybody can see that."

At this point Nem approached, trailed by his daughter. "Your boy is asking for trouble," the staffer told him. "Hig don't want to hurt him, but—"

"He's of age," Nem said regretfully. He was not a large

8

man himself, but the assurance with which he wore his sword suggested his size in the circle. "He wants his manhood. I can't deny him longer."

"See?" Neq demanded, smirking. "You prove your stick on me, before you prove anything on my sister."

All three men stiffened. That had been a nasty jibe. Now Hig the Stick would have to fight, for otherwise Nem himself might challenge him to keep Nemi chaste. It was no secret that the sworder was protective toward both his children, but particularly toward his pretty daughter.

Hig approached the circle, drawing his sticks. "I gotta do it," he said apologetically.

Nemi sidled near. "You idiot!" she whispered fiercely at Neq. "I was only fooling."

"Well, *I* wasn't!" Neq replied, though now he felt shaky and uncertain. "Here is my weapon, Hig."

Hig looked at Nem, shrugged, and came to the white ring. He towered over Neq, handsome and muscular. But he was not an expert warrior; Neq had watched him fight before.

Hig stepped inside. Neq came at him immediately, covering his nervousness with action. He feinted with his blade in the manner he had practiced endlessly, emulating the technique of his father. The sticker jumped away, and Neq grinned to show greater confidence than he felt. It had actually worked!

He drove at Hig's middle while the man was catching his balance. He knew that thrust would be blocked, and the next, but it was best to maintain the offensive as vigorously as possible. Otherwise he'd be forced to the defensive, which did not favor the sword. Especially against the quick sticks.

But he scored.

Adrenaline had made him swift. The sword thrust inches deep into Hig's abdomen. The man cried out horribly and twisted away—the worst thing he could have done. Blood welled out as the sword wrenched loose. Hig fell to the ground, dropping his sticks, clutching the gaping mouth in his belly.

Neq stood dazed. He had never expected it to be this easy—or this gruesome. He had intended the thrust as another ploy, braced to get clipped a few times while he searched for a genuine opening. To have it end this way—

"Hig yields," the staffer said. That meant Neq could leave the circle without further mayhem. Ordinarily the man who remained in the circle longest was the victor, regardless what happened inside, since some were clever at feining injury as a tactical ruse, or at striking back despite wounds.

He was abruptly sick. He stumbled away from the circle, heedless of the spectacle he made. He retched, getting vomit in his nose. Now, calamitously, he understood why his father had been so cautious about the circle.

The sword was no toy, and combat was no game.

He looked up to find Nemi. "It was awful!" she said. But she was not condemning him. She never did that when the matter was important. "But I guess you won. You're a man now. So I fetched this from the hostel for you."

She held out a gold bracelet, the emblem of adulthood.

Neq leaned against her sisterly bosom, crying. "It wasn't worth it," he said.

After a while she took a cloth and cleaned him up, and then he donned the bracelet.

But it *was* worth it. Hig did not die. He was packed off to the crazy hospital and the prognosis was favorable. Neq wore the invaluable bracelet clamped around his left wrist, proud of its weight, and his friends congratulated him on his expertise and assumption of manhood. Even Nemi confessed that she was relieved to have had her liaison with the sticker broken up; she hadn't liked Hig that well anyway. She could wait for womanhood— *weeks*, if need bel

10

There was a manhood party for Neq, where he announced his name, which was duly posted on a hostel bulletin board for the crazies to record. There was no eligible girl in this group, so he was unable to consummate his new status in the traditional fashion. But the truth was that he was as leary as was his sister of the actual plunge. Man-man in the circle was straight-forward. Man-woman in the bed . . . that could wait.

So he sang for them, his fine tenor impressing everyone. Nemi joined him, her alto harmonizing neatly. They were no longer technically brother and sister, but such ties did not sever cleanly at the stroke of a sword.

A few days later he commenced his manhood trek: a long hike anywhere, leaving his family behind. He was expected to fight, perfecting his craft, and to move his bracelet about, becoming a man of experience. He might return in a month or a year or never; the hiatus would establish the change of circumstance, so that all nomads would respect him as an individual. Never again would he be "Nem's kid." He was a warrior.

It was a glorious moment, this ceremony of departure, but he had to hide the choke in his throat as he bid farewell to Nem and Nema and Nemi, the family he had set aside. He saw tears forming in his sister's eyes, and she could not speak, and she was beautiful, and he had to turn away before he was overcome similarly, but it was good.

He marched. The hostels in this region were about twenty miles apart—easy walking distance, but not if a man tarried overlong. And Neq tended to tarry, for many things were new to him: the curves and passes of the trail, unfamiliar because he had never seen them alone before, and the alternating pastures and forests and the occasionally encountered warriors. It was dark by the time he found his first lodging.

And lonely, for the hostel was empty. He made do for himself, using the facilities the crazies had provided. The crazies: so-called because their actions made no sense. They had fine weapons that they did not use, and excellent food they did not eat, and these comfortable hostels they never slept in. Instead they set these things out unguarded for any man to take. If everything were removed from a hostel, the crazies soon brought more, with no word of protest. Yet if a man fought with his sword outside the circle reserved for combat, or slew others with the bow, or barred another from a hostel, and if no one stopped him, the crazies cut off their supplies. It was as though they did not care whether men died, but how and where. As though death by arrow were more morbid than death by sword. Thus there was only one word for them: crazy. But the wise warrior humored their foibles.

The hostel itself was a thirty-foot cylinder standing as high as a man could reach, with a cone for a roof. Somehow the cone caught the sunlight and turned it into power for the lights and machines within. Inside there was a fat column, into which toilet facilities and food-storage and cooking equipment were set, and vents to blow cool air or hot, depending on the need.

Neq took meat from the freezer and cooked it in the oven. He drew a cup of milk from the spout. As he ate he contemplated the racks of bracelets, clothing, and weapons. All this for the taking without combat! Crazy!

At last he pulled down a bunk from the outer wall and slept, covering his head from the stillness.

In the morning he prepared a pack with replacement socks and shirt, but did not bother with extra pantaloons or jacket or sneakers. Dirt did not matter, but the items that became sweatsoaked did need changing every so often or discomfort resulted. He also packed bread and the rest of the meat: waste was another thing the crazies were sensitive about, despite their own colossal waste in putting this all out for plunder. Finally he took a bow and a tent-package, for he intended to do some hunting and camping on this trek. The hostels were fine for occasional use, but the typical nomad preferred to be independent.

The second night he camped, but it was still lonely and he had forgotten to take mosquito repellent. The third night he used a hostel, but he had to share with two other warriors, a sworder and a clubber. It was friendly, and they did not talk down to him though they had to be aware of his youth. The three practiced in the circle a bit, and both men complimented Neq on his skill: meaning he still was a novice. In serious combat no compliments were needed; the skill spoke for itself.

The fourth night he found a woman. She prepared a meal for him that was immeasurably superior to his own makings, but did not make any other overtures, and he found himself too shy to proffer his bracelet. She was as tall as he, and older, and not really pretty. He took a shower in her presence so she could see he had hair on his genital, and they slept in adjacent bunks, and in the morning she wished him good fortune in a motherly fashion and he went on. And cursed himself for not initiating his bracelet, at the same time knowing he was even more afraid of somehow mishandling it and being ridiculed. How could a man feign experience in such a matter?

The fifth day he arrived early at a hostel set near a beautiful small lake, and a man was there. By his fair, unblemished features he was not much older than Neq, and he was not substantially larger, but he had the bearing of a seasoned warrior.

"I am Sol of All Weapons," he announced. "I contest for mastery."

This set Neq back. Mastery meant the loser would join the tribe of the winner. Because it was a voluntary convention, it did not violate the crazies' stricture against deprivation of personal freedom, but a man honor-bound was still bound. Neq had only fought once and practiced some, and didn't trust his luck in serious combat. Not so soon, anyway. He didn't want to join a tribe so soon, and had no use for a tribe of his own.

"You use all weapons?" he asked, putting off the implied challenge. "Sword, staff, sticks—all?"

Sol nodded gravely.

"Even the star?" He glanced at the morning star maces on the weapons rack.

Sol nodded again. It seemed he wasn't much for conversation.

"I don't want to fight," Neq said. "Not for mastery. I—I just achieved my manhood last week."

Sol shrugged, amenable.

About dusk a woman showed up. She wore the sarong of availability, but she was if anything less young and less pretty than the one Neq had met before. She must have borrowed many bracelets in her time, yet no man had retained her. Sol paid her no attention; he was without his own bracelet, showing he was married. So it was up to Neq again—and again he did nothing.

The woman prepared supper for them both, as this was the function of the available distaff. She had the same assurance about her cooking that Sol did about his weapons. This must be her territory, so that she was used to catering to any men who came here, hoping that some would prefer capability to beauty and would leave the bracelet on her. No woman ever took her bracelet directly from the rack; it had to come from a man.

Before the meal was served, a third man arrived. He was a large warrior, paunchy, gruff, with many scars. "I am Mok the Star," he said.

"Sol of All Weapons."

"Neq the Sword."

The girl said nothing; it was not her place. She made another setting at the table.

"I contest for mastery," Sol said.

"You have a tribe? This boy and who else?"

"Not Neq. My tribe is training in the badlands."

"The badlands!" Mok's surprise matched Neq's own. "No one goes there!"

"Nevertheless," Sol said.

"The kill-spirits—"

"Do you question my word?" Sol demanded.

Mok bridled at the tone. "Everyone knows—"

"I have to agree," Neq said—and was immediately aware that he had spoken out of turn. This was not his quarrel.

"In the *circle* you challenge my word!" Sol said. He glanced at the rotating transparent door, noting that it was dark outside. "Tomorrow."

Mok and Neq exchanged glances. Both were stuck.

"Tomorrow," Mok agreed. "For mastery." Then as an afterthought: "But you will see my weapon is not for games."

The girl smiled at Mok. He smiled back, stroking his bracelet. And that night Sol and Neq pulled down bunks from the wall on the east side, while Mok took the woman to the west side, putting his bracelet on her wrist.

Neq lay in the dark, listening, feeling guilty for it. But he couldn't really tell anything from the sounds.

Sol had a barrow filled with weapons. "What would you face in the circle?" he asked Mok.

"You really use then all? Let's have the star, then."

Sol brought out his ball and chain. Neq was fascinated. He had never seen a star in action, and had never heard of a star-star encounter in the circle. The weapon was unreliable but terrifying, as it could not be used defensively. Either the heavy spiked ball connected or it didn't, and the outcome of the battle depended on that. Serious injury was a probability, in this match.

There was a personal consolation: if Sol were injured, Neq would not have to fight.

The two men entered the circle on opposite sides, each whirling his deadly steel ball over his head so rapidly that the short chains were blurs. Now the stars were beautiful, flashing the sunlight in rings of fire as the men's torsos flexed rhythmically. The fight had to be short, for the outward pulling weight of the ball would rapidly tire the arm.

It was short. The two bright arcs intersected, the

15

chains crossed, the balls spun about each other fiercely, striking sparks. Both Mok and Sol jumped as their chains yanked—but it was Sol who hung on to his star. Mok's handle slipped from his grasp, and he was disarmed.

Neq realized that this was exactly what Sol had intended. He had deliberately engaged the other weapon, not trying for the man at all, and had jerked sharply the moment contact was made. Mok had expected the entanglement to interfere with both warriors, so that he could use his weight to advantage in the clinch. Sol's strategy and timing had been superior.

Or could it have been sheer luck?

"What would you face?" Sol asked Neq.

Already! Not the star, certainly! Was it courtesy or confidence the man showed? What to answer!

A sword or dagger in a skilled hand could hurt him severely, like Hig. The sticks were blunt, but the pair of them could rattle his brain. The club was blunt and slow, but a real mauler when it connected. The staff—

"The staff!" One piece, slow, no edges, safe.

Sol calmly brought out his staff.

They entered the circle and sparred. Neq felt guilty for his cowardice. A real warrior would have chosen to oppose his own weapon, so the threats were equal. The quarterstaff was safe, but hard to circumvent. Neq feinted—

When he came to, his head was throbbing. He was on a bunk in the hostel. The woman wearing Mok's bracelet —Moka—was sponging his face.

Neq refrained from asking what had happened. Obviously he had been felled by a blow he had never seen. Could Mok have struck him from behind? No—that would have been a gross violation of the circle code, and there had been no evidence that either Sol or Mok were the type to practice or tolerate such dishonor. The staff must have passed his guard—

He touched his head. The welt reminded him. An astonishingly deft maneuver, the staff avoiding his sword as if it were fog, whipping in—ouch!

Well, he was a member of Sol's tribe now. The badlands tribe. If there were kill-spirits there, they hadn't
hurt Sol much! On balance, it wasn't such a bad outcome.
Nem had always said there were advantages to serving a
strong leader. What a man lost in independence he
gained in security. Provided he joined a good tribe.

Neq wasn't quite confident he had joined a good one,
for there remained some doubt whether Sol was an excellent warrior or merely lucky. But Neq put the best face
on it: would he have let himself be taken by a fluke?

He traveled with Mok, following instructions, while Sol
continued in the opposite direction. Mok had reclaimed
his bracelet after the second night, and Neq didn't question him. Maybe the man just didn't care to take a wife to
the badlands, though Sol said the kill-spirits—he called
them roents—had gone back beyond the camp. They
were on the trail several days.

Sol's tribe, or at least the portion of it they joined,
seemed to consist of about thirty men encamped in and
about another hostel under the general eye of his wife
Sola. She was a sultry beauty of about sixteen, inclined to
sharpness when addressed and brooding silence at other
times. But she wore her gold bracelet proudly.

For two weeks they tarried there, their numbers aug-
mented by other converts Sol sent back. A number of
men had families, so that the drain on the supplies of the
hostel was considerable. They hunted with bow and
arrow in the forest to supplement those waning rations,
though twice the crazy van came to restock them.

The crazies were as funny in person as their name
indicated: strangely garbed, unarmed, almost devoid of
muscle, and ludicrously clean. Yet their truck was a monster, capable of crushing many warriors if misdirected.
Why should they act like servants to the nomads, when
they could so easily assume power? Some thought it was
because the crazies were weak and foolish, but Neq
doubted that it could be that simple.

Eventually Sol returned with another fifteen men,
swelling the tribe to over fifty. Then the whole group

17

marched—to the badlands. Neq viewed the red crazy warners with alarm, knowing they marked the boundaries of the kill-spirits as surveyed by the crazy click boxes. But nothing happened.

A camp had been established in the wilderness beside a river, with a flooded trench around it. The leader of this camp was Tyl of Two Weapons; but the man who really ran it was Sos the Weaponless. Sos drilled the men mercilessly, setting up subtribes for each weapon and ranking each man according to his skill. Neq began as the bottom sworder of twenty, chragrined, but he prospered under the training and rose eventually to fourth of fifty. The camp was growing all the time, as Sol traveled and sent more warriors. There was no doubt of the tribe's power now; he had never seen such discipline.

Strange that it was all the doing of a man who would not fight in the circle himself. Sos obviously had an enormous store of information about combat, and he was no weakling physically. Yet he kept a stupid little bird on his shoulder, the ridicule of all the tribe, and obviously loved Sola without admitting it. Neq once saw her go to his tent in winter and stay there until dawn. The whole situation was incredible.

When spring came, the tribe was ready to move out as a unit, and Neq was a ranking member. He was eager for the promised conquest.

Only one thing marred his success: he had not yet had the courage to offer his bracelet to a girl. He wanted to, but he was not yet fifteen, and looked thirteen, and a live naked woman was just too much for him to contemplate. The mistakes he might make!

Sometimes he dreamed of Sola. It wasn't that he loved her, or even liked her; it was that she was a lusciously constructed female who stayed in another man's tent though her husband was master of the tribe. Dishonor . . . but excruciatingly tantalizing! She was the kind to keep a secret. . . .

That was one reason he had improved so much as a

sworder: he spent almost all of his free time practicing, while others allowed themselves to be diverted by romantic concerns. They thought him dedicated, but he was tormented.

Some day—some day he would really be a man!

CHAPTER TWO

Neq prospered in battle, too, winning his matches easily. His first match was against the first sword of a smaller tribe. The other master had not wanted to fight, and Neq had been one of the carefully picked hecklers who taunted him into a commitment. His opponent in the circle was good, and Neq was so nervous he feared his weapon would quiver—but incredibly his intensive winter's training had made him better. Sos had drilled him until he was furious, not only against swords but against all other weapons, and had matched him in pairs with others to fight other pairs. It had been tedious, hard work, and since the practice sessions were never for blood he had only Sos's opinion to certify his actual skill. But that opinion was justified; as Neq saw the little crudities of the other man's technique he knew it was all true. Clumsy victories and confused losses were no longer Neq's lot. He really *was* a master sworder, not far behind Tyl himself, who was first.

Then, suddenly, Sos the Trainer left. It was an ironic question who mourned his departure more: Sol or Sola. Had Sol found out? But the tribe continued operating as Sos had organized it. Sola birthed a baby girl, though nine months before her husband had been away a great deal. . . .

The tribe became so large through conquests that it had to be broken up into ten subtribes formed into an empire. One was under Sol and the others under his major lieutenants: Tyl of Two weapons, who had the finest warriors; Sav the Staff, who took over the badlands camp as a training area and was the other songsinger of the empire; Tor the Sword, with his great black beard . . . and, gratifying, Neq himself. Each subtribe went its own way, acquiring more warriors, but all were subject to Sol ultimately.

At first it was wonderful, for Neq's fondest dreams of glory had been exceeded. He was chief of a hundred and fifty warriors, which was more than most independent tribes boasted. He visited his family and showed off his status. His sister had married and moved away, but hometown doubters he gladly convinced. He packed half a dozen of them off to the badlands camp, and even demonstrated his skill against his father Nem, though not for blood or mastery. Neq was the finest sworder this area had ever seen, and it was good to have it known.

But in a year such things palled, for administrative duties kept him from practicing in the circle as much as he liked, and there seemed to be rivalries and enemies on every side. He decided that he was not, at heart a leader. He was a fighter.

By the end of the second year he was heartily sick of it, but there seemed to be no way down the ladder. He longed just to run away by himself, meeting people honestly, without the barrier his present responsibility erected.

And—he still wanted a woman. He was sixteen now, more than man enough—but the very notion of offering his bracelet to a girl, any girl, filled him with dread. If one would ask *him*, make it clear she was amenable . . . but none did.

Neq suspected that he was the shyest man in all the empire—and for no reason. He could command men without qualm, he could meet any weapon with confidence, he could run a tribe of hundreds. But to put his bracelet on a woman . . . he *wanted* to, but he *couldn't*.

Then disaster came to the empire. A nameless, weaponless warrior appeared—one who entered the circle and defeated the empire's finest *with his bare hands*. It seemed impossible—but the Nameless first took Sav's tribe, breaking Sav's arm; then Tyl's tribe, shattering Tyl's knees; then Tor's—by killing Bog the Club, the one warrior even Sol had not beaten. And finally he brought Sol himself to the circle, and took all the enpire and Sola too for his own, sending Sol to die with his girlchild at the mountain.

Neq's tribe had been ranging far from the scene of that action, and by the time he got there the issue had been settled and Sol was gone. There was nothing for him to do but go along with the new Master. Tyl remained second in command, acting in the name of the grotesque Weaponless conquerer, who seemed to have little interest in the routine affairs of empire. "Go where you will," Tyl advised Neq privately. "Battle where you will. But no more for mastery. Query your warriors and release any who wish to leave, asking no questions. The Nameless has so decreed."

"Why did he conquer, then?" Neq demanded, amazed.

Tyl only shrugged, disgusted. Neq knew Tyl much preferred Sol's way—but he was a man of honor to match his station, and would not act against the new Master.

So it came to pass. For six years the empire stagnated. Neq turned over his administrative duties to other men and took to wandering alone, incognito. Sometimes he fought in the circle—but his blinding skill with the sword made such encounters meaningless, and destroyed his alias. And still his bracelet had never left his wrist, though he dreamed of women, all women.

At the age of twenty four, with a decade of nomadic brilliance behind him, Neq the Sword was over the hill. He had no present and no future, like the empire.

Then the Master invaded the mountain, using his own and Tyl's subtribes—and disappeared. Tyl returned with news that the mountain fortress had been gutted; that the men who went there in the future really *would* die, whatever had been the case in the past. But Tyl could not claim the leadership of the empire. No one had defeated the Weaponless. He might or might not return.

The chiefs met—Tyl, Neq, Sav, Tor and the others— and formally suspended the empire, pending that return. Each subtribe would become a full tribe, but they would not fight each other.

Neq wanted only freedom, so he dissolved his own tribe completely. The top warriors immediately began forming their own tribelets and moving out. Neq, truly independent for the first time in his life, wandered alone again.

The third time he came to a lodge in a hostel and found it gutted and broken, Neq grew perplexed and angry. Who was doing this, and why? The hostels had always been sacrosanct, open for all travelers all the time. When one was destroyed, every person suffered. Too much of this would hurt the entire nomad society—that had supposedly been saved by the razing of the mountain underworld.

There was no hope of catching the perpetrators; the deed was weeks past. Easier to inquire of the crazies themselves, who were often knowledgeable about nomad affairs but who never acted positively.

Neq, missionless until this moment, had found a mission of a sort.

The local crazy outpost was under siege. Its foolish glass windows had been broken in, and now fragments of wood and metal furniture barred them ineffectively. The flower beds around the building had been trampled. Two unkempt warriors patrolled in semicircles at a distance, one on either side, and three more chatted around a nearby campfire.

Neq accosted the nearest of the marchers, a large sworder. "Who are you and what are you doing?"

"Beat it, punk," the man said. "This is private soil."

22

Neq was not young or impulsive any more. He replied calmly: "It looks to me as though you are molesting a crazy outpost. Have you any reason?"

The man drew his blade. "This is my reason. Got it clear now, shorty?"

Neq saw that the others had been alerted, and were coming at a run. They were all sworders. But he held his ground. "Are you challenging me in the circle?"

"Hey, this guy's a troublemaker!" the man cried, amused.

"Cut off his balls—if he has any!" one of the others said, approaching with weapon drawn.

Neq was assured by this time that these were noncircle outlaws: clumsy fighters who banded together informally to prey on whoever was helpless. Such wretches had never been tolerated within the crazy demesnes before, and the empire had systematically run them down and executed them. That is, they were forced to meet a capable warrior in the circle, contesting for life. There was no sense in having the crazies halt maintenance because of the actions of outlaws.

But the empire was gone now, and the weeds were encroaching. He would have no compunction about cutting down such cowards. Still, he made sure: "Give me your names."

They ringed him now. "We'll give you a bleeding gut!" the first man said, and the rest chuckled.

"Then I give you mine. I am Neq the Sword." He drew his weapon. "The first to move against me defines the circle."

"Hey—I've heard of him!" one man cried. "He's dangerous! Got a tribe—"

But already the others, no students of the empire heirarchy, were closing in, thinking to overwhelm him by their dishonorable mass attack.

Neq swung into action the moment they moved. He thrust ferociously at the one directly in front, driving his point into the man's unguarded chest and yanking it out

23

again immediately. Then he whirled the bloody blade to the left, catching the next man at the neck before he could raise his sword in defense. Such tactics would never have worked against competent warriors—but these were combat oafs. He swung right, and this man had his guard up, so that sword clanged on sword.

Neq leaped away, passing between the two bleeding men. Two remained, for the fifth had fled after recognizing him. Neq spun to face them as they looked at their fallen comrades, appalled. Novices frightened of blood!

"Take your wounded and get out of here," he snapped at them. "If I see you again, I kill you both."

They hesitated, but they were inept cowards and he knew it. He turned his back on them contemptuously and went to the outpost building. He knocked on the door.

There was no answer.

"The siege is lifted," he called. "I am Neq the Sword— Warrior of the circle. You have me in your records."

Still silence. Neq knew that the crazies kept track of all the nomad leaders, and had duplicate dossiers.

"Stand before the window," a voice called at last.

Neq walked to the shattered window. He saw that the rough sworders were stumbling away with their comrades.

"There *is* a Neq-sword listed," another voice said. "Ask him who his father is."

"Nem the Sword," Neq answered without waiting for the question. These crazies! "And my sister is Boma; she took Bom the Dagger's band and bore two boys by him."

"We have no record of that here," the second voice said after a pause. "But it sounds authentic. Did he serve in the nomad empire of Sol of All Weapons?"

"Bom? No. But if you saw my action of a moment ago, you know *I* served."

"We have to trust him," the first voice said.

Neq returned to the door. There was the sound of laboriously shifting furniture. Keys. It opened.

Two old men stood within. They were typical crazies:

24

cleanshaven, hair shorn, parted and combed, spectacles, white shirts with sleeves, long trousers with creases, stiff polished leather shoes. Ludicrous apparel for any type of combat. Both were shaking visibly, obviously unused to personal duress and afraid of Neq himself.

"How did you hold them off?" Neq asked, genuinely curious. A nomad in such decrepit condition would begin excavating his cairn.

One crazy picked up a vaguely swordlike instrument. "This is a power drill, operating off house current. I turned it on and put it against any part of the body that entered the building. It was sickening but effective."

"And we do have weapons," the other said. "But we aren't adept at their use."

Obviously. "How long has this been going on?"

"For two days. We've had similar attacks recently, but our supply trucks were able to disperse them. This time the truck did not come."

"Probably ambushed, boarded and wrecked," Neq said. "I found three gutted hostels too. But those jackals never had the nerve to attack you before. What's the reason?"

"We don't know. Supplies have been short, and we have not been able to stock our hostels sufficiently. The nomads seem to have been making war against us."

"Not the nomads! Those were outlaws!"

They peered at him dubiously. "We don't question your values, but—"

"My values aren't hurting," Neq said. "You have evidence that regular warriors are rampaging against you?"

"It seems so."

"But that's suicidal! We are not completely dependent on the hostels, but they do make possible a special way of life. Their sanctity has always been honored."

"So we thought. But as you have seen—"

Neq sighed. "I have seen. Well, I want you to know that I do not condone this destruction, and I'm sure most nomads agree with me. How may I help you?"

25

The two exchanged timid glances. "Would you be willing to bear a message to our main depot?"

"Gladly. But the way things are going, you need protection here. If I go, you won't survive long."

"We can not desert our post," one man said sadly.

"Better that than death," Neq pointed out.

"It is a matter of principle."

He shrugged. "That's why you are called the crazies. You *are* crazy."

"If you will carry the message—"

"I'll take the message. But first I think I'd better see to your defenses. I can round up a few men—"

"No. We have never worked that way."

"Crazies, look," Neq exclaimed, exasperated. "If you *don't* work that way now, your post will surely and shortly be a smoking hole, and you buried under it. You have to take some note of reality."

"A compelling case," the man admitted. "You have obviously had tactical experience. But if we do not function according to our philosophy, we have no point in functioning at all."

Neq shook his head. "Crazy," he repeated, admiring their perverse courage. "Give me your message."

The main post was a school. The message was for one Doctor Jones, and he meant to deliver it personally to the man.

A blonde crazy girl sat at a desk as though guarding her master from intrusions. "And who is calling?" she asked, her professional eye analyzing him comprehensively. She was quite clean, and that was mildly annoying too.

"Neq the Sword."

"N E K or N E G?"

He merely stared at her.

"Oh, illiterate," she said after a moment. "Dr. Jones will see you now."

He entered the interior office and handed over the written message. The aged, balding crazy within broke the seal immediately and studied the scribbled sheet of paper. He looked grave. "I wish we had been able to install telephonic cables. So our trucks have not been getting through?" he obviously knew the answer.

"Those two men are probably dead by now," Neq said. "Crazies just won't listen to reason. I offered to protect them, but—"

"Our ways differ from yours. Otherwise we would be nomads ourselves—as many of us have been, in youth."

"You were a warrior?" Neq asked incredulously. "What weapon?"

"Sword, like you. But that was forty years ago."

"Why did you give it up?"

"I discovered a superior philosophy."

Oh. "Well, those crazies at the outposts are *dying* by their philosophies. You'd better call them in."

"I shall."

At least the crazy master had some sense! "Why is this happening? Attacks on your posts, hostels—it was never this way before."

"Never in your memory, perhaps. I could give you an answer, but not a completely satisfactory one." Dr. Jones sat behind his desk and made figures with his hands. He had long spindly wrinkled fingers. "We have been unable to supply the hostels properly in recent months. Normal attrition thus reduces some of these to virtual uselessness for travelers. When that happens, some men react adversely—and, lacking the stability of civilization, they strike out senselessly. They are hungry, they want clothing and weapons—and none are available. They feel they have been unfairly denied."

"But why can't you supply them anymore?"

"Because our own supplies have been cut off. We are chiefly distributors; we do not manufacture the implements. We do have a number of mechanized farms—but food is only part of our service."

"You get the weapons and things from somebody else?" Neq had not realized this.

"Until recently, yes. But we have had no shipments for

several months, and our own resources are practically exhausted. So we are frankly unable to provide for the nomads, with the unfortunate results you have noted."

"Didn't they tell you what happened? Your suppliers, I mean?"

"We have had no contact. Television broadcasts ceased abruptly, so there seems to have been a severe power loss. Our supply trucks have not returned. I fear that now the very restlessness our lapse promotes is rebounding against us: a feedback effect. The situation is serious."

"Your whole hostel system will break down?"

"And, I am very much afraid, our schools and hospitals and farms. Yes. We cannot withstand the concerted attacks of so many armed men. Unless we are able to resolve this matter expeditiously, I have grave reservations about the stability of our society in its present form."

"You're saying we're all in trouble?"

Dr. Jones nodded. "You are succinct."

"What you need is someone to go find out what's wrong at the other end. Someone who can fight. If your truck drivers are like the men I met at the outpost—"

Jones nodded again.

"*I'll* go, if you like."

"You are most generous. But you would not be conversant with the details. We would require a written report—"

"I can't write. But I could guard a literate."

Jones sighed. "I will not claim your offer is unenticing. But it would be unethical for us to use you in this fashion. And you might have difficulty protecting a 'crazy'."

"You're right. I can't help a man who won't listen."

"So I thank you for your service in bearing this message." Jones stood up. "You are welcome to remain with us for as long as you desire. But I doubt that you are inclined toward the quiet life."

"I doubt it's quiet anymore," Neq said. "But it does differ from my—my philosophy." He put his hand on the hilt of his sword. "By this I live."

28

"Doctor."

Both men glanced over to see the blonde girl in the doorway. "Yes, Miss Smith?" Dr. Jones said in his question-statement tone.

"I listened over the intercom," she said, looking rebelliously guilty. "I overheard Mr. Neg's offer—"

"Neq," Neq said, pronouncing it carefully. "Neq the Sword."

"With a Q, I'm sure," Jones said, smiling. "One of the most skilled of the nomad swordsmen today."

Neq was startled, for Dr. Jones had given no hint of his information before. But of course an ex-sworder would keep track of such things, and Neq was in the crazy records.

"I could go with him," Miss Smith said, and a flush came to her rather pretty features. "I haven't entirely forgotten the wild life—and I could make the report."

Jones looked pained. He had an excellent face for it. "My dear, this is not the type of enterprise—"

"Doctor, you know our whole structure will collapse if we don't do *something*!" she cried. "We can't go on much longer."

Neq stayed out of this debate, watching the girl. She was young but quite attractive in her animation. Her two breasts were conical under her light crazy sweater and her skirted legs were well proportioned. She was worth a man's contemplation despite her outlandish attire. He had heard that "Miss" applied to a crazy woman signified her eligibility for marriage; they used words instead of bracelets.

Jones faced Neq. "This is somewhat awkward—but she is technically correct. Our need is imperative, and she would seem to be equipped to do the job. Of course it is not incumbent on you to—"

"I can guard a woman as easily as a crazy man," Neq said. "If she'll do what I say. I can't have her standing on 'principle' when a warrior's charging us."

"I'll do what you say," she said quickly.

"My mind is not easy," Jones said. "But we *do* require the information. Even a negative report—which I very much fear is to be anticipated—would enable us to make positive plans to salvage a very limited sphere. If both of you are amenable—"

Neq considered more carefully. How far would he travel in a day, fettered to this doll-pretty crazy woman? She would faint at the sight of blood, surely, and collapse before they had walked sixty miles. And the ridicule he would evoke, marching with a crazy companion, *any* crazy, but particularly a *female* crazy—

"It wouldn't work," he said. And felt a certain familiar frustration, knowing that his shyness with women had as much to do with it as logic.

"It *has* to work," she said. "Dr. Jones can do amazing things, but only if he has exact information. If you're worried about my keeping up—we'll take a truck. And I don't have to look this way. I'm aware of your contempt. I can dress like a nomad. I'll even put on some dirt—"

Jones almost smiled, but Neq shrugged as though it wasn't that important to him. If they didn't get there, they didn't get there. The notion of traveling with a handsome woman, even a crazy, had its subtle but developing appeal. This was business, after all; his private problem could not be permitted to interfere. "All right."

"All right?" She looked surprised.

"Put on some dirt and get your truck and we'll go."

She looked dazedly at Jones. "All right?"

Dr. Jones sighed. "This is against my better judgment. But if both of you are willing—"

CHAPTER THREE

The change in blonde Miss Smith was amazing. She had unbound her hair to wear it loose and long in nomad fashion, and she had the one-piece wraparound of the available. Gone was the crisp office manner: she spoke only when addressed, knowing her place in the presence of a warrior. Had Neq not known her origin, he would have been fooled. Of course his close experience with women was meager.

She, however, had to drive the truck. Neq had seen the crazy vehicles on occasion, but had never actually been inside one before. The handling of such machinery was not his forte, obviously. So he rode beside her in the cab, sword clasped between his knees, and clung to the seat as the wheels bumped over the ruts. The velocity of the thing was appalling. He kept expecting it to start panting and slow to a walk, for no one could run indefinitely! He had been told a truck could cover in one hour a distance equivalent to a full day's march, if it had a good track, and now he believed it.

The road was no pleasure. What suited for foot traveling became hazarous for wheels, particularly at this speed, and he was privately terrified. Now he understood why the crazies had always been so fussy about the maintenance of their trails, cutting back the brush and removing boulders. Such natural obstacles were like swinging clubs to the zooming vehicle. Neq refused to show it, of course, but his hands were clammy on the sword and his muscles stiff from tension.

But in time he became acclimatized, and watched Miss Smith's motions. She controlled the truck by turning a wheel around: when she pushed the top of it north, the truck swung north. When she wanted to stop she pushed a metal pedal into the floor. Driving was not so difficult after all!

All day they drove, stopping only to let Neq be sick from the unaccustomed motion, and to refuel. The first was mortifying, but Miss Smith pretended not to notice and in time his gut became resigned. The second was just a matter of pouring funny smelling liquid she called gasoline into the motortank from one of the large metal drums carried in the back. "Why don't you just pipe it in from the drums?" he asked, and she admitted she didn't know.

"These trucks were designed and probably built by the Ancients," she said. "They did a number of inexplicable things—like making a gas tank far too small for a day's driving. Maybe they *liked* pouring gas from cans."

Neq laughed. "That's something! To the crazies, the Ancients are crazy!"

She smiled, not taking offense. "Sanity seems to be inversely proportional to civilization."

Inverse proportion: he knew what that meant, for he had been drilled like the others in the empire training camp. They had used numbers to assess combat ranking: the smaller the number, the higher the warrior stood.

They drove on, until they had to stop to do patchwork on the road. A gully had formed, the result of some cloudburst, and made a tumble of boulders of the road-bed. Here Neq felt useful, for Miss Smith could not have budged all those rocks or shoveled enough sand into place to make the passage.

Despite these delays, Neq estimated that they had come a good five days march by dusk.

"How much do you normally march?" she inquired in response to his remark.

"Thirty miles, alone. More if I'm in a hurry. Twenty, with a tribe."

"So you make it a hundred and fifty miles today."

He worked it out, counting off fingers. He knew how to count and calculate, but this was a different problem than the type he normally encountered. "Yes."

"Speedometer says ninety-four," she said. "It must have seemed faster than it was. On a paved road it would have been double that."

"The truck keeps track of its own travels?" he asked, amazed. "Maybe it forgot to count the section between the tank-filling and the roadwork."

She laughed again. "Maybe! Machines aren't bright."

He had neither worked with nor talked with a woman

this way before, and was surprised to realize that it wasn't difficult. "How far is this supplier?"

"About a thousand miles from the school, direct. Somewhat farther by these backwoods trails."

He figured again. "So we have about ten days of travel."

"Less than that. Some areas are better than others. Let me show you our route on the map. I think we've been through the worst already."

"No."

"No?" She paused with the map in her hand.

"The worst is what stopped your other trucks from returning."

"Oh." She was prettily pensive. "Well, we'll find out. The others didn't have an armed guard along."

She opened the map and pointed out lines and patches of color to him, but it was largely meaningless to Neq, who could not relate to the continental scope of it. "I can find the way back, once I've been there," he said.

"That's good enough." She studied the map a bit more, then put it away with a small sigh.

There were canned and even frozen goods. Miss Smith lit a little gas stove and heated beans and turnip greens and bacon, and she opened the little refrigerator and poured out milk. Neq had never had a woman do for him on a regular basis, and this was an intriguing experience. But of course she only looked like a woman; she was a crazy.

They slept in the truck—he in the back beside the gas drums, she curled in the cab. She seemed to feel there would be something wrong if they both slept in the back, though there was far more room there and she had to know that no honorable nomad would disturb her slumber without prior transfer of the bracelet. She could not know, of course, that Neq had never had relations with any woman. The only girl he had been close to was his sister. In fact, had Miss Smith not been a crazy, he would

33

have been extremely nervous. As it was, he was only moderately nervous, and relieved to sleep alone.

But in his dreams women were ubiquitous, and he was not bashful. In his dreams.

The second day of travel was uneventful, and they made almost two hundred miles. The novelty of riding in the truck palled, and he stared moodily into the rushing brush and covertly at Miss Smith's right breast, shaped under the cloth as she steered. She seemed less like a crazy, now.

He began to hum to his sword, and when she did not object he sang to it: the folk songs he had picked up from happy warriors like Sav the Staff, in the glad days of the empire's nascence.

Oh, the sons of the Prophet were hardy and bold
And quite unaccustomed to fear.
But the bravest of all was a man so I'm told
Named Abdullah Bulbul Ameer.

The references were meaningless, as were the names, but the melody always brought pleasure to him and he responded to the warrior mood of such songs. From time to time he was tempted to change the words a bit, adapting to the things he knew, but that forfeited authenticity. "Oh, the warriors of empire were hardy and bold . . ." No—songs were inviolate, lest they lose their magic.

After a time he realized with a shock that she was singing with him, in feminine harmony, the way Nemi used to do. That jolted him back into silence. Miss Smith made no comment.

The third day they encountered a barricade. A tree had fallen across the road.

"That isn't natural," Neq said, alert for trouble. "See— it has been felled, not blown. No nomad cuts a tree and leaves it."

She stopped the truck. In a moment men appeared—

34

unkempt outlaws of the type he had encountered before. "All right, you crazies—out!" the leader bawled.

"You stay here," Neq said. "This will be unpleasant for you. Maybe you'd better duck down so you can't see." He got out in one bound and lifted his weapon. "I am Neq the Sword," he announced.

This time no one recognized the name. "You think you're pretty smart, dressing like a man," a big clubber said. "But we know you're crazies. What's in your truck?"

Miss Smith had not followed his suggestion. Her pale face showed in the cab window. "Hey!" the leader cried. "This one's a lady-crazy!"

Neq advanced on his man. "You will not touch this truck. It is under my protection."

The man laughed harshly and swung his club.

He died laughing.

Neq let him drop and moved to the next, a scarred dagger. At the same time he watched for bows, for outlaws were capable of anything. He would have to perform some deft maneuvers if arrows came at him. "Run," he suggested softly.

The dagger looked at the bleeding clubber corpse and ran. That was the thing about outlaws: they were easily frightened.

Neq charged the leader, another dagger. This man, at least, had some courage. He brought up his knives and sliced clumsily.

It was axiomatic that a good dagger would lose to a good sworder when the combat was serious. This man was not good, and Neq cut him down immediately.

No one else remained. "Scream if you see anything," he told Miss Smith. "I'm scouting the area." He had to be sure that all the teeth of the ambush had been drawn before he tackled the fallen tree.

She just sat there, her features stiff. He had known she would not like it. Crazies and women were similar in that respect, and she was both.

He located the outlaw camp. It was empty. The

35

cowardly dagger had lost no time spreading the word. From the traces there had been at least two women and four men. Well, now it was two women and *two* men—and he doubted they'd attack any more trucks.

He went back. "It's clear," he told Miss Smith. "Let's haul this trunk out of our way."

She seemed to wake, then. He surveyed the tree and decided it was too much for him to move without cutting in half. He made ready to hack at it with his sword, but Miss Smith called to him. "There is an easier way."

She brought out a rope and hitched it to the base of the tree trunk. Then she looped the other end into the front bumper of the truck. Then she started the motor and backed the vehicle away slowly until the tree was dragged out lengthwise along the road. Neq gaped with a certain confused respect.

She brought a peavy from the back. He limbed the tree and used the tool to roll the main mass clear of their path. This was still heavy work, but far more efficient than his original notion.

He wound the rope and put the peavy away. They got back into the cab. "Let's move," he said gruffly.

She drove mechanically, not looking at him.

"You surprised me," he said after a while. "I never thought of using the truck like that."

She didn't answer. He glanced at her, and saw her lips thin and almost white, her eyes squinting though the light was not strong.

"I know you crazies don't like violence," he said defensively. "But I warned you not to look. They would have killed us if I hadn't wiped them out first. They didn't set that ambush just to say hello."

"It isn't that."

"If we hit any more bands like that, it'll be the same. That's why your trucks aren't coming back. You crazies don't fight. You think if you're nice to everyone, no one will hurt you. Maybe once that was true. But these outlaws just laugh."

"I know."

36

"Well, that's the way it is. I'm just doing the job I promised. Getting the truck through." Still he felt awkward. A man would have understood, even a crazy man. Maybe. "I was sick myself, the first time I fought a man and wounded him. But you get used to it. Better than getting hit yourself."

She drove for a while in silence. Then she braked the truck. "I want to show you something," she said, her face softening.

They got out under the shade of spreading oak trees. She stood before him, breathing rapidly, her yellow hair highlighted momentarily by a stray beam of sunshine. She was as pretty a girl as he had seen, in that pose. "Come at me."

Neq was abruptly nervous. "I meant no offense to you. I only tried to explain. I have never attacked a woman."

"Pretend you're an outlaw about to ravish me. What would you do?"

"I would *never*—"

"You're shy, aren't you," she said.

It was like a blade sliding wickedly through his defense. Neq stood stricken.

Miss Smith shook her hand—and there was a knife in it. No lady's vegetable parer—this was a full-length warrior's dagger, and her grip on it was neither diffident nor clumsily tight. There was a way of holding that was a sure signal of circle readiness, and this was her way.

Instantly Neq's sword was in his hand, his eye on the other weapon, his weight balanced. One never ignored a blade held like that!

But Miss Smith did not attack. She unwrapped her wraparound, revealing one firm fresh breast, and tucked the knife into a flat holster under her arm. "I just wanted you to understand," she said.

"I would never have struck you," he said, numbed by both her weapon-readiness and the glimpse of her torso. But it sounded ridiculous, for there he stood with sword ready. He sheathed it quickly.

"Of course not. I checked your file, once I got your

37

name straight. You were a tribal chieftain, but you never took a woman. What I meant was: understand about *me*. That I was wild once. I'm not really a crazy. Not when it counts."

"You—used the dagger?"

"When I saw you fighting those brutes—the blood—it was as though a dozen years had peeled away, and I was the gamin again. I found the knife in my hand, there in the cab."

"Twelve years! You fought as a small child?"

Her mouth quirked. "How old do you think I am?"

"Nineteen." It was an unfortunate fact that most married women lost their beauty early. At fifteen they were highly desirable; ten years later they were faded. The unmarried lacked even that initial freshness. Miss Smith was obviously not in the first bloom, but still pretty enough.

"I am twenty-eight, according to Dr. Jones' best estimate. No one knows for sure, since I had no family."

Three years older than Neq himself? That was incredible. "Your breast says nineteen."

"When I was nineteen—" she said, mulling it over. "When I was nineteen, I met a warrior. A strong, dark man. Maybe you know of him. Sos—Sos the Rope?"

Neq shook his head. "I knew a Sos once, but he had no weapon. I don't know what happened to him."

"I would have gone nomad with him—if he had asked me." She thought for a moment, still breathing quickly. "I would have gone nomad with anyone."

This was all awkward, and Neq's hands were clammy, and he didn't know what to say.

"I'm sorry," she said. "It was the blood, the action—it made me react in an uncivilized way. I shouldn't have shown you."

"I thought you were sick. In the cab."

"I was. Emotionally. Let's forget it."

They climbed back into the truck, but he didn't forget it. He kept trying to coincide that ripe breast with her

38

advanced age. What secret did the crazies have, to preserve a woman so?

And her knife. That motion had been swift and sure. She *had* run wild once; such talents were not readily come by, and a woman did not carry a weapon unless she knew how to use it.

Dr. Jones had said that many crazies including himself had once been nomads. This was one such.

They stopped and had a supper heated on the engine —that saved time and fuel—before he brought himself to the point. "Why did you come with me?"

"The real reason? As opposed to the one I claimed?"

He nodded.

"I suppose I still crave what I can't have. A way of life, a—a freedom from responsibility. A—a man."

A half-pleasant chill went through him. "There are crazy men."

"A *man*," she said with emphasis. "Like you."

"Are—are you asking for my bracelet?"

Even in the dusk he could see the flush rise to her face, and he hoped his own cheeks were not betraying him as mercilessly. "A woman doesn't ask."

His heart was beating, and suddenly he desired her intensely despite her age and her crazy ways. She *had* asked, in her fashion, and she was more approachable than the women he had encountered before. Perhaps because of the very things that had seemed to put her beyond any such connection. A literate, knife-bearing, twenty-eight year old crazy!

He had come to know her as a person before seriously considering her as a potential sex object, and that made a considerable difference. Three days . . . and that was longer than he had known any other woman this intimately . . . except Nemi.

"I never gave my bracelet—even for a night."

"I know. But I don't know why."

"I—was afraid of being refused." He had never spoken this truth before. "Or that it wouldn't work."

39

"Would that be so bad? To—fail?" Now he could see her pulse actually making the clothing quiver rhythmically. She was as wrought up about this conversation as he was. That helped, in a way . . . and hurt, in another way.

"I don't know." It made no sense, intellectually, for he could face defeat in the circle without such shame. But with a woman, his fear seemed insurmountable.

"You are handsome enough, strong enough," she said. "I don't think I've seen a more comely nomad. And you sing beautifully. I don't think you would be refused."

He studied her yet again, comprehending her meaning. It was darker now, but his night vision illuminated her more clearly than ever. He was shivering with tension and incredulous passion. Slowly he reached his right hand over to his left wrist, touching the gold band there.

She did not move. Her eyes were on his hands.

He grasped the bracelet, twisting. It slid about his wrist but did not come away. He would have to spring it out a little, for that. But his hand would not cooperate.

Miss Smith watched him, the flush remaining on her face. It enhanced her beauty.

Neq forced his fingers apart as though he were straining at hand-wrestling and hooked them into the open section of the band. Slowly he applied pressure. Sweat trickled down his neck. His arm jerked nervously.

At last he got the metal off. His wrist felt naked, cold. He lifted the bracelet, seeing the sweat marks on it. He wiped it ineffectively on his shirt, trying to make it clean. Then, inch by inch, he carried it toward her.

Miss Smith raised her left hand. Unsteadily their two arms came together. The gold touched her wrist.

And she snatched her arm away. "No—no—I can't!" she cried.

Neq was left with his bracelet extended, refused. It was the very thing he had feared, all these years.

"Oh Neq, I'm sorry!" she said. "I didn't mean it like that. I didn't know this would happen."

40

Neq remained with the bracelet extended, his eyes fixed on it. He didn't know how he felt.

"It isn't what you think," she said. "I—I'll take it. The first shock . . ." She raised her wrist again . . . and dropped it. "I *can't*!"

Slowly Neq brought the band back to his own arm, and clasped it there.

"I'm ashamed," she said. "I never thought—please, don't be angry."

"I'm not angry," he said around a thick tongue.

"I mean—don't feel rejected. It's me, not you. I never —I—I'm worse than you. Oh, that sounds awful!"

"You never had a man?" Neq discovered that analyzing her problem was much easier than doing something about his own.

"Never." She forced a laugh. "If I had been a normal nomad, I'd be a grandmother by now."

Not far from the truth. "Not even this Sos?"

"I don't think he was ever really aware of me. He had some nomad woman on his mind; that's why he came to the school."

"I guess it's all right," he said after a pause.

"I don't understand." She spoke more freely now that the crisis had passed.

"I didn't really want to give you my bracelet. I just wanted to see if I could do it. So that I wouldn't have to see myself as a coward."

"Oh."

He saw that he had been cruel. And it had been a lie. "I don't mean that I don't want *you*. It's the—the principle." Now he sounded like a crazy himself, and it was still a lie. "It's that you're old—older than I am. And a crazy."

"Yes." Yet she was *not* a crazy, not exactly. And had she been a full nomad, he would not have been able even to proffer his bracelet, ironically.

And her simple agreement to his lies and his half-lies made it worse. "You don't *look* old. If you hadn't told me—"

41

"Can't we let it drop?"

He should have been silent from the start. It would have spared her needless shame and improved his own image. He had failed—not in proffering the bracelet, but in trying to talk about it.

So the matter dropped—but not very far.

CHAPTER FOUR

Next day it rained steadily. They tried to keep driving, but the trail became so mushy that the wheels were in obvious peril. If they became mired here today, they might not get out tomorrow. Miss Smith pulled up on the crest of a low hill and parked.

"We have a long wait," she said. "It will take at least a day for those ruts to firm up again."

Neq stared out at the steady rain and shrugged. It was not that rain bothered him, but it was an inconvenience generally and a hindrance to this mission. He might have gone foraging in the forest and checked out the local lay of the land, but he couldn't leave Miss Smith here alone. Her knife would not help much if outlaws attacked the truck again.

"Well," she said with a certain artificial brightness. "Shall we try it again?"

Neq looked at her, uncertain of her meaning.

"We're stuck here together for some time," she explained. "We both need the experience. Yesterday was bad, but I think I'm stronger now. If we keep trying, maybe—"

Oh, the bracelet! "Right now? Here?"

"Maybe day is better than night. Fewer spooks. Have you anything better to do? Or did you mean it, about not—"

42

"No!" To both questions.

"Maybe if we do it quickly, we won't balk."

Suddenly the idea appealed to him. He was sorry for the way he had insulted her before, and she was giving him a chance to make it right. She carried no grudge. His sweat was only beginning; if he treated the matter like circle combat, acting automatically, he might do his part before she could work up too much fear to do hers.

He clapped his hand on his bracelet, jerked it off, thrust it at her. She met him halfway.

Their wrists banged. The bracelet fell to the floor.

"Oh, *damn!*" she cried, using the crazy expletive. "I'll get it. She reached down just as Neq did. Their heads bumped.

Embarrassed, he began to laugh.

"It's not funny," she said. "I'm trying to find the—"

Impulsively he caught her by slim shoulders and hauled her upright. He brought her face to his and kissed her.

There was no magic in it. Her lips, taken by surprise, were mushy. The bracelet dangled from her fingers.

"Put it on," he said. "I think we'll make it."

She looked at the gold, then back at him.

Something struck the cab on her side.

"Down!" Neq barked. He was already in motion, ducking, flinging open the door, tumbling to the muck near the wheel. Sword in hand, he crouched by the truck, watching for the enemy.

He had recognized the striking arrow by the sound. That meant outlaw attack. Probably not well organized, because they had parked randomly, but no matter to be taken lightly.

He was right. Through the rain he heard two men talking. They were debating whether to approach the vehicle now, or try more arrows first. They had not seen the door open.

They decided to charge. "Those crazies can't fight," one said. "Just yank it open and haul them out."

43

They came up, touched the driver's door—and Neq charged them from the side. The battle was brief. In a moment two bodies lay in the mud.

"Let's go," he called to her.

"Go?" She pushed open her door. "We can't move the—"

"Not the truck. Us. Where there are two, more may be on the way. We can't stay in the obvious target."

She jumped down, one foot striking one of the corpses. She moved away quickly.

They were not dressed for the rain, but did not tarry. He led her into the forest, away from the truck. Neither spoke.

Neq found a gnarly yellow birch and climbed it, searching out a suitable perch that would be hidden from the ground. Miss Smith followed, and he put her astride one fat round limb. He took another. Water poured down their backs, but this was a good defensive situation just in sight of the truck.

They waited that way for three hours.

A man came—an ugly clubber. He passed about thirty feet from their tree, evidently searching for someone.

He discovered the truck, and what lay beside it. He ran back. He was alone. Neq jumped down. "Hey, outlaw!"

The man swung to face him, club lifted.

"I killed them," Neq said. "As I shall kill you, if you don't—"

The clubber was no coward. He charged Neq, swinging viciously. That was all Neq needed to know. A true nomad would have protested the designation of "outlaw" and demanded satisfaction in the circle. He would not have attacked like this.

Neq ducked the blow and slashed in return. He wanted this one alive. There was information he needed.

The clubber swung again. This time Neq parried, sliding his blade down along the shaft of the club until it nipped the man's hand. Not a serious wound, but

44

enough to convince the man he was overmatched. As, indeed, he was.

"Tell me what I want to know, and I let you go."

The clubber nodded. Neq backed off, and the man relaxed. Miss Smith remained hidden in the tree, wisely; it was best that the outlaw not know of her presence.

"If you lie to me, I will take up your trail and kill you," Neq said. "But I would not take the trouble—except for vengeance."

The clubber nodded again. Vengeance was something even outlaws understood well. The man might betray Neq if he had the chance, but he would be exceedingly careful about it. He would certainly answer questions honestly.

"How many in your tribe?"

"Twelve. Ten, now. And their women."

"All outlaw?"

"No. We're a regular tribe. But we take what offers."

"And if a crazy truck comes, you take it too?"

"Not before this. That must've been Sog's idea. If he saw it stopped, mired—"

"And your chief doesn't care?"

"He has to eat too. The hostels don't stock any—"

"Because the trucks are being raided!" Neq said. "The crazies can't stock the hostels when their trucks are hijacked."

"I can't help that," the clubber said sullenly.

Neq turned away in disgust, hoping the man would strike at him from behind and justify a killing return thrust. But the clubber stayed honest, perhaps aware of the trap.

"Go tell your chief to stay away from this truck," Neq said finally. "I'll kill anyone who comes near."

The man left.

Neq made sure he was gone before returning to the tree. "Do you think that will work? Miss Smith asked him. She was shivering, but that would be from the wet chill.

"Depends on the chief. If he's a full outlaw, he'll try to swamp us. If he's halfway nomad, he'll let us be."

"Then why did you let that man go? Now the tribe will know where we are."

"I want to know what's really stopping those trucks. This is one way to find out."

- She climbed down stiffly. Her garment was clinging to her torso and she was blue with the cold. "I wish there were an easier way."

"There isn't. If I hadn't stopped him, he would have brought the tribe to the truck anyway. If I had killed him, the others would have come looking. No tribe can let its members just disappear. It was better to give them warning."

"This could happen any time any truck stops," she said. "Are *all* the nomads outlaws now?"

"No. I'm not. But if only one man in five is, no truck will get through."

"They're so quick to turn against their benefactors!"

Neq shrugged. "As the club said: they have to eat."

"I didn't think it would be like this."

"We'll go back to the truck."

"But that's where they'll attack, if—"

"That's why we have to be there, now. I'll set some traps and keep watch; you can sleep."

"I can't sleep, waiting for them to come!"

"Then I'll sleep while you keep watch," he said, heading back to the vehicle.

He hauled the men away from the side and left them near the yellow birch as a reminder to approaching tribesmen. Then he checked the cab. "Where's my bracelet?"

She flushed. "I—" She poked her arm out of the sodden cloth. The bracelet was on it, far back because of the much smaller girth of her forearm, but there.

"You put it on!" he said, amazed.

"There wasn't anything else to do with it, when you jumped out," she said defensively.

46

"All right, Neqa. Sing out if you see anything."

"I'll give it back!" she said. "I didn't mean—"

"You meant. Let it stay. It's never been on a woman before."

"But I still can't—"

"Do you think *I* can? But I'd like to. Maybe after a few days." Oddly, he wasn't sweating, though of course he was completely wet. *She* was on the defensive now, not he.

"Yes," she said. "That would be nice."

"I'll squeeze it tight for you." He took her limp arm, slid the band down to her wrist, and applied his thumbs to the heavy metal ends. The gold gave way, and slowly the bracelet constricted to match her size.

"Euphemism makes it so much easier," she murmured. "Thank you." She was still shivering, though it was warm in the cab. She was afraid, all right—of outlaw attack, of the meaning of a man's band on her arm, of indecision. She needed protecting.

"I never was kissed before . . ." she said, as though nothing had happened in the interim.

Had he done that? Suddenly he felt as though a sword had grazed his scalp, and he was weak with reaction.

Neq lay in the back of the truck and slept, ignoring the continuing drizzle. He was a warrior; he could sleep anywhere, regardless of the weather. Miss Smith—Neqa pro tem—needed the shelter of the cab.

He dreamed. He had treated the transfer of his bracelet lightly, but it was fundamental. For the first time a woman had accepted it, and they were married, however tenuously. The rest would surely follow. That was his dream, and all of it: a lovely woman bearing his bracelet, loving him.

"Neq!"

He woke immediately, sword ready. She was right: there were men approaching the truck. In the face of his warning there could only be one reason, and no mercy.

Silently he dropped from the back and flattened himself against the side. He identified the marauders by their sounds: they were clumsy stalkers. Six, seven, eight or more.

It was dusk—bright in the sky yet, but dark under the trees. An advantage for him, for he could strike anywhere, while they had to watch for each other.

Neq wasted no time. He ran noiselessly at the nearest, a sworder. The man was dead before he realized the fight had started. Neq took his place and stalked the truck with the others. Nothing showed in the cab. Good—Neqa was staying down.

"See anything?" a clubber whispered as they converged. "That guy is dangerous."

It was the man Neq had warned before. He walked up as though to whisper a reply—and ran his point into the man's neck so that he died without a cry.

But the group had converged too much for further secrecy. "That's him!" someone cried.

Then Neq was lashing out, dancing here and there, cutting down whatever he could reach and jumping away in a fury of swordsmanship. Six men hemmed him in— two sworders, two clubbers, a staffer and a dagger. It was the staffer he was most cautious about, for that weapon could interfere with his action while the others closed in. He retreated toward the truck.

Two more men ran out of the forest and climbed on the truck. "Neqa—defend yourself!" Neq cried. Beset as he was, he could not go to her himself.

One man yanked open the door. "A woman!"

He reached in, then fell back, grunting. Neq knew she had used the knife. In the cramped space of the cab, it would be more effective than a sword.

The cab door swung closed, and the second man backed away from it, joining the main force. Seven warriors remained to the tribe, and now they knew the limits of their opposition. The element of surprise was gone. Neq had hoped to do more damage before it came to this. Had it been down to three or four functional

48

enemies, in the near-dark, he could have brought them down. But seven threw the balance against him unless they were extraordinarily clumsy or unlucky. He could dodge and run, but he couldn't fight them long without getting hurt himself, and ultimately killed.

Then the motor of the truck started. It roared, and the blinding headlights came on. She was going to try to drive it away!

But the truck backed and turned, its rear wheels spewing up gouts of wet earth. The lights speared toward him. The motor roared again, like some carnivorous animal at bay, and the vehicle bounced toward the group of men.

She wasn't going to stop! Neq threw himself to the side, out of the path of the great rubber tires. Mud and sand sprayed at him.

Not all the outlaws were as quick to realize the danger. They hadn't ridden this machine for three days, and didn't respect its potential. They stared, confused.

The front bumper caught two, not striking them hard enough to kill at this slow speed, but knocking them down. One screamed horribly as the wheel went over him. The other scrambled to safety, only getting clipped on the foot.

In the confusion Neq clove a sworder across the face, and one more was down. *Two* more, counting the one under the wheel. He retreated again, but did not go far from the truck.

The huge machine crashed into a tree, shattering a headlight. The wheels spun, digging holes. The gears growled. Then it backed, lifting out of its own trench in one mighty contortion.

Neq ran to it and jumped on the back. A clubber, catching on, tried to follow him. A backhand slash dispatched that one.

Back across the road they went, slowing in the deepening mud, and the remaining outlaws scattered. The single headlight caught one; the gears howled again, and the truck jumped forward toward that man. He fled to the side, waving his two sticks. The bright beam followed him.

Neq had not until that moment appreciated the fact that *the truck was a weapon.* A terrible one, for no man could stand against it, even though its footing was treacherous in this rain. Miss Smith—*Neqa!*—was making it a living, ravening monster, spreading terror and carnage within its limited domain.

Back and forth the one-eyed creature went, hurling mud behind, lurching at any moving thing its light caught, bumping over the bodies in the road. One man was buried face-down in that dark pudding of mud, only his legs clear. To and fro endlessly, as though hungry for more.

And the enemy was gone. Five of the tribe's number were dead, and Neq knew that others were wounded, the rest intimidated. The battle was won.

The truck stopped. The motor died, the headlight went off. Neq climbed down and went around to the cab.

"Is that you, Neq?" she called. He saw the small glint of her blade in the lingering light of the dashboard.

"Me." He climbed in.

"Oh God!" And she was sobbing like any jilted nomad girl. Neq put his arms about her and pulled her across the seat to his chest, and she clung to him in her sudden misery of relief.

"I was so afraid they'd attack the tires!" she said.

"No, they only attacked me."

"Oh!" she cried, beginning to laugh. It was stupidly funny, somehow.

She had his bracelet, she was in his arms, she was overflowing with reaction and need . . . but that was as far as it went. This was not the time.

CHAPTER FIVE

The following day he sang again, as the sun came down and steamed the forest floor into solidity. He pretended to sing to his weapon, but it was really to her, and she knew it.

> I know my love by her way of walking
> And I know my love by her way of talking
> And I know my love by her suit of blue—
> But if my love leaves me, what will I do?

"You sing very well," she said, reddening a bit.

"I know it. But it isn't all real. When I sing of battle, I know what it means. But love—those are words I don't understand."

"How do you know?" It was as though she were afraid to ask, but was fascinated anyway.

He looked at his bare wrist. "I never gave my—"

She held up her own wrist with the heavy gold bracelet clasped about it. "You gave. I accepted. Is that love?"

"I don't know." But he was breathing jerkily.

"Neq, I don't know either," she admitted. "I don't feel different—I mean I'm still *me*—but the gold seems to burn, to lead me along, I don't know where. But I want to know. I want to give—everything. I'm trying to. But I'm old, and crazy, and afraid. Afraid I have nothing *to* give."

"You're beautiful, and warm, and brave. That business with the truck—"

51

"I hate that! Being a killer, I mean. But I had to do it. I was afraid for you."

"That must be love."

"I like the sound of that. But I know better, Neq. I could hate you and still need you. If anything happens to you, I have no way home."

That was the wonder of it: she was as afraid of him as he was of her. She fought rather than see him hurt—yet she could not come to him in peace. She had to impose practical reasons to justify what needed no justification. As he did, too. "Show me your breast," he said.

"What?" She was not shocked, only uncomprehending.

"Your knife. Your—when you put away your knife, you—"

"I don't understand." But she did.

"Show me your breast."

Slowly, flushing furiously, she unwrapped her shoulder, exposing her right breast.

"It is nineteen," he said. "It excites me. A breast like that—it *can't* be old, or crazy, or afraid, or have nothing to give. It has to be loved."

She looked at herself. "You make me feel wanton."

"I will sing to your breast," he said.

She blushed again, and her breast blushed too, but she did not cover herself. "Where do you learn these songs?"

"They go around. Some say they come from before the Blast, but I don't believe that." Yet he did believe it as much as he disbelieved it, for so many of the words made no sense in the nomad context.

"The books are that old. The songs might be." Her flush was fading at last.

He sang, contemplating her breast:

Black, black, black is the color
    of my true love's hair.
Her lips are something rosy fair.
The prettiest face and the neatest hands
I love the ground on where she stands.

She blushed yet again. "It's so real when you sing like that. I'm glad my hair's not black."

"Are you?" He was vaguely disappointed.

"No. I wish the song *did* fit."

"Enough fits. All except the hair."

"Does it?" She looked hopeful.

"No. I'd like it to fit." After a pause he added: "Neqa."

She couldn't seem to stop blushing. "You make me all confused when you say that. Neqa."

"Because of the bracelet."

"I know. I'm your wife as long as I wear it. But it isn't real."

"Maybe it will be." If only it were that simple!

"You nomads—you just pass the bracelet and that's it. Instant love, for an hour or a lifetime. I don't understand it."

"But you were a nomad once."

"No. I was a wild girl. No family. The crazies took me in, trained me, made me like them, outside. They do that with anyone who needs it. I never was part of the nomad society."

"Maybe that's why you don't understand the bracelet."

"Yes. What about you?"

"I *understand* it. I just can't *do* it."

"Maybe that's the trouble with us. You're too gentle and I'm too timid." She laughed nervously. "That's funny, after we killed all those men. Gentle and timid!"

"We could hold each other tonight. It might help."

"What if the outlaws come back?"

He sighed. "I'll stand watch."

"You watched last night. I should do it this time."

"All right."

She laughed again, more easily, so that her breast moved pleasantly. "So matter of fact! What if I said 'take me in your arms, crush me, make love to me!'?"

He considered the prospect. "I could try. If you said it before I got too nervous."

"I can't say it. Even though I want to."

"You want to do it—but you can't ask me?"

"I can't answer that." This time she forgot to blush.

"I want to do it," he said seriously. "But I can't just start. Not unless you say. And even then—"

"It is funny, you know. We know what we want, we know how each feels, but we can't act. We can even speak about speaking, but we can't speak."

"Maybe tomorrow," he said.

"Maybe tomorrow." And the look of longing she gave him as she put away her breast made his heart pause and jump.

Tomorrow was another clear day, and the ruts were hardened, and there seemed to be the first whiff of something from the corpses around the truck, and so they moved out. Nature compensated for the day's delay by providing an excellent route.

That night Neqa joined him in a double sleeping bag in the back of the truck and pressed her breast against him, but she did not ask and he did not do. They both were frustrated, and they talked about it, and they agreed the whole thing was ridiculous, but that was all.

They had to keep alert against possible marauders, so they took turns sleeping even though together, and while she slept he tried to touch her breast with his hand but didn't . . . but it was against his hand when he woke after her turn awake.

The next night they slept together naked, and he ran his hands over both her fine breasts and her firm buttocks, and she cried when she could not respond, and that was all.

The night after that he sang to her and kissed her, and she ran her hands over his torso and did not avoid what she had avoided before, huge as it was, and she pressed against him and he tried . . . but she cried out with a pain that might have been physical and might have been emotional, and he stopped, chastened, and she cried quietly for some time.

Meanwhile, they were making much faster progress

toward the supplier. Their union unconsummated, they pulled up to a hostel near what Neq recognized with shock as the mountain: the place of nomad suicide. Gaunt rusty girders projected from it, hiding the summit; he knew that no man who had passed that barrier had ever returned . . . until recently.

Yet Tyl of Two Weapons and the Master had laid siege to this bastion, for there had been living men within it. They had gutted it, and now it was truly dead.

Neqa consulted her map. "Yes, this is it."

"This—your supplier?" he demanded.

"Helicon. But something is wrong."

"We destroyed it," he said. "The Weaponless did, I mean; I was not there. I could have told Dr. Jones, if I'd known he was talking about the mountain!"

"Oh, no!" she cried. "Helicon manufactured all the technical equipment! We cannot do without it!"

"Maybe some are alive, inside." Knowing Tyl's efficiency, he doubted it, but he had to offer her some hope.

She moved around the center column of the hostel, looking for something. This hostel had not been ravaged, but there was no food in it. She opened the shower stall and stepped in.

"You're still dressed," Neq reminded her.

"I know it's here," she said, as though he hadn't spoken. "I memorized the instructions." She counted tiles along the wall, then pressed on one. She counted from another direction and pressed again. And once more. Nothing happened.

"You have to turn the knobs," he said. "One for hot, the other for cold. But you don't need to take a shower right now, just when you're beginning to smell like a true nomad—"

"I must have done it too slowly," she said. "Now I know the tiles, I'll try it faster."

She went through her mysterious ritual again, while Neq watched tolerantly. The crazies were crazy!

Something snapped inside the inner wall. Neqa pushed

55

on yet another tile and it tilted out, revealing a handle. Neq gaped; he had never known there were handles behind the shower wall! If not for hot or cold water, what?

She twisted and gave a sharp jerk—and the entire wall swung toward her.

There was a compartment behind the shower—in the heart of the hostel's supposedly solid supporting column!

"Come on," she said, stepping inside.

Neq joined her, clasping his sword nervously. There was barely room for them both. She pulled the wall shut and touched a button inside. There was a hum; then the floor dropped.

Neq jumped, alarmed, but she laughed. "This is civilization, nomad! It's called an elevator. We have them in our buildings, and the underworld uses them too. This is a secret entrance, that we use for transfer of supplies. When nomads see a crazy truck outside, they assume it's a routine servicing—but the truth is we're taking supplies *out*. Most of the heavy stuff comes through other depots in the area, of course, that the nomads never see."

The floor stabilized. She pushed open the side again, and now there was a tunnel, curving into darkness.

"Bad," she said. "The lift is on hostel power, that charges whenever the sun shines. But the tunnel is on Helicon power. That means the underworld is dead, as you said." She turned on a flashlight Neq hadn't known she possessed. "But we'll have to look."

The passage opened into a room where empty boxes were stacked. "Someone's been here," she remarked. "They took the merchandise. But the crates were never restored."

"Probably the last truck—that didn't return."

"Our men never went beyond this point," she said. "But obviously there is a passage to Helicon. We'll have to find it."

"It may not be pretty." He had heard the tales of labyrinthine underground tunnels choked with bodies. Such claims were probably exaggerated; still. . . .

"I know it." She kissed him—she was able to do that now, and was proud of herself—and began pushing again at places in the wall, randomly.

"If they didn't want you inside, it wouldn't open that way," he pointed out. "Might even be booby-trapped."

"I don't think so. They might guard it, but they wouldn't do anything to antagonize us. The crazies, I mean. Helicon needed us as much as we needed it, because they'd largely shelved their hydroponics and couldn't grow really decent vegetables, and of course no wood. It was more efficient to trade with us, so they concentrated on the heavy industry we couldn't touch. Dr. Jones can talk endlessly about such things—what he calls the essential interactions of civilization."

"So it's safe to break in, you think," he said.

She continued to tap at panels without effect. Neq studied the wear-marks on the floor, analyzing their pattern as though he were verifying the situation of a vacated campsite. "There," he said, touching one section of the wall. "It opens there."

She joined him at once. "Are you sure? This seems solid."

He pointed to the floor marks her flash illumined, and she understood. With this hint, they were able to locate a significant crevice. "But it doesn't open inward," he said. "No hinge on this side, no scrape-marks."

"I don't find any other crease," she said. "But it has to open somehow." She banged at the corner with the butt of the light. "Unless it slides—"

Neq forced the point of his sword into the crevice and leaned on it. The wall gave a little, sidewise. "It slides—but it's locked or blocked."

"Naturally it would lock from the other side," she said. "Can you free it?"

"Not with my sword. But we can get a crowbar from the truck. Enough leverage, it'll give."

They returned to the vehicle and collected an armful of tools. And in due course they had it open.

Behind the wall was a set of tracks. "They used a railroad!" she said. "To haul the supplies along, maybe by remote control. How clever."

But there was no wheeled cart, so they had to walk between the tracks. Neq was nervous about this, not liking the confinement, but she didn't seem to mind. She took his hand in the dark and squeezed it.

He counted paces. It was over a mile before the tracks stopped. There were platforms, with boxes stacked, and sidings with several carts. Neq opened one crate and discovered singlesticks—perhaps fifty of the metal weapons.

So it was true: the underworld had made the nomad arms. Hadn't the Weaponless known that when he destroyed it?

They walked along to the end of the platform and passed through a dark doorway. Then up a gradual ramp, through a charred aperture, and into a larger hall. The air was close and not sweet. Neqa passed the beam of the flashlight over the floor.

Ashes lay across it, with occasional charred mounds. The ambient odor was much stronger here.

"What happened?" she inquired, perplexed.

Neq saw that she didn't comprehend. "Fire. They couldn't get out in time."

"*They*?" Then she recognized the shape of the nearest mound and screamed. It was the remains of a human being.

Neq led her back down the ramp. "See—after they were dead, the wooden door finally burned through. It must have locked or jammed, like the panel back there. Someone must have poured gasoline all over everything and—"

She turned to him in the darkness, the flashlight off. "The nomads did this?"

"Tyl said it happened before they broke in, actually. The fires were still hot, and the smoke was everywhere, so they didn't stay long. I don't know."

58

She made a choking sound. He felt something warm on his arm, and knew that she was vomiting against him.

"Helicon was the last hope of man!" she exclaimed, and heaved again.

"I don't think we need to look any more," he said. He took the flashlight from her flaccid hand and guided her away.

CHAPTER SIX

Neqa insisted on writing her report. "In case anything happens, this will tell the story," she explained. "Also, I'm sure of the details now. I hope I forget them by the time we get back."

They slept in the truck that night, though the hostel bunks were handy. The tunnel connection to the Helicon carnage was too direct; it felt as though the fumes of death were filtering along, enclosing the hostel in their horror. Neq had been objective about the scene at the time, but at night his imagination enhanced the underworld's gruesomeness. Fresh death in the circle, or fighting outlaws—that was one thing. But this helpless doom of confined fire. . . .

There was no question of trying to make love. They clung tightly together, holding the morbid blackness off.

Next day Neqa completed her report and locked it in the dash compartment of the truck. They moved out. Neq still didn't see any reason for a written description; the place was dead, and that was it. Such a message would hardly be any comfort to the crazies. They would be finished anyway, and the nomad culture would degenerate into complete savagery.

What colossal folly had led the Weaponless to lay siege to Helicon? He had brought it down, somehow—but had destroyed both the crazies and the nomads with it. The dark age of man was beginning.

Neqa didn't say much either. He was sure that similar thoughts were obsessing her. If information was all they had come for, the mission had been successful. But what a miserable mission it was!

The second day of the return trip they encountered a barricade that had not been there before. Neq was instantly on guard; this surely meant trouble.

"Coincidence?" Neqa inquired.

"Can't be. They saw us go by before, knew we would have to come back this way. So they set it up."

They had to stop. There was no way around, no room to turn.

"If we're lucky, they won't have more than a guard or two here right now. They wouldn't know exactly when we might come along," he said.

They were not lucky. Men converged from both sides. Sworders, clubbers, staffers—at least a score of warriors. A number stood back with drawn bows.

"Do you think this is where the other trucks were lost?" she inquired as though it were an interesting footnote for her report.

"Most of them. This is well organized." He studied the situation. "Too many to fight. And if we try to back out now, those arrows will get us. See, they're aiming at the tires. We'll have to go along—as far as we can."

A sworder strode up to Neq's side. "You're a warrior. What are you doing in a crazy truck?"

Before Neq could reply, a man called from the other side: "Hey, this one's a woman!"

"What luck!" another exclaimed. "Is she young?"

"'Bout nineteen."

"OK. Out, both of you!" the sworder said.

Neq was furious, but glanced again at the bows covering them and dismounted. No honest nomad would use the hunting bow against a man, but that didn't diminish its effectiveness as a long-distance weapon. Neqa slid over to step down on his side. She stood close to him, but clear of his sword, so as not to obstruct his draw. He knew she was ready to snap her dagger into her hand: she was tense.

"Know what I think?" the sworder said. "I think they're crazies, both of them, pretending to be nomads. They want us to think they hijacked the truck themselves, so we'll leave 'em be. See, her hands are smooth, and he's too small to really handle a sword. And unmarked—no scars on him."

"Pretty smart," a staffer said.

"The crazies are awful smart—and awful stupid."

"All right, crazy," the sworder said. "We'll play this game. We got the time. Who do you claim to be?"

"Neq the Sword."

"Anybody hear of any Neq the Sword?" the man shouted.

There was a reaction. "Yeah," a dagger said.

"Me too," a clubber agreed. "In Sol's tribe. A top sworder—third or fourth of a hundred swords, I heard. And better against other weapons."

The sworder smiled. "Crazy, you picked the wrong name. Now you'll have to prove it—in the circle. With your doll watching. And if you can't—"

Neq didn't answer. The circle was exactly where he wanted to be—with Neqa in sight. These were certainly outlaws, but the tribe seemed to be large enough to require the discipline of the circle code. It was a matter of logistics: one tough man could control five or ten warriors by force of personality on an informal basis, and a few more by judicious intimidation; but when the number was thirty or forty, it had to be more formal. The circle code was not purely a matter of honor; it was a practical system for controlling large numbers of fighting men in an orderly fashion.

And where the circle code existed, even imperfectly, Neq could prevail. He had indeed been third or fourth sword of a hundred. But first sword had been Tyl, who had retired largely to managerial duties of empire. Second had been killed in a noncircle accident. Third had been Tor, now retired. And Neq had kept practicing. The result was that at the time of the breakup of the empire he had been unofficially conceded second sword—of three thousand. And he had had private doubts about Tyl's continuing proficiency in the circle.

It was true, too that the empire training had brought particular competence in inter-weapon combat. There had been half a dozen staffers who could balk Neq in the circle, one or two stickers, Bog the Club who was now dead, and no daggers or stars. Against these men he would take his chances, sometimes prevailing in friendly matches, sometimes not.

Neq feared no man in the circle.

They were conducted to a camp similar to those of the empire. A large canvas tent was surrounded by a number of small tents, and there were separate latrine, mess, and practice sections. A good layout.

The chief of this tribe was a huge sworder, grizzled and scarred. Chiefs were generally sworders, for the weapon had a special quality that awed others into submission that an equally competent staff could not. When the man stood, he towered over Neq.

"Neq the Sword, eh? I am Yod the Sword. And she wears your band?"

"Yes."

"Now I know of Neq," Yod said. "Maybe the top sworder of the empire, a few years back. He never gave his bracelet to a woman. Isn't that strange?"

Neq shrugged. The chief thought he was toying with the captive.

"Well, all shall be known," Yod said. "I shall give you the tour."

And a tour it was. "I have fifty excellent warriors," Yod said, gesturing to the tent. "But for some reason we're short of young women, and that makes the young men restive. So the girl will have a place with us, regardless."

Neqa walked closer to Neq and let her bracelet show, defensively.

"I have supplies enough for many months," Yod boasted. "See."

Four crazy trucks were parked behind the main tent. There was no longer any doubt who was the main hijacker. But it made little difference, since Helicon was dead.

"And entertainment." Yod gestured to a hanging cage.

Neq looked at this curiously. There was a man inside, huddled within a filthy blanket. Metal cups lay on the wire floor, evidently for his eating, and ordure had cumulated underneath. Apparently they did not release him even for natural functions. He had room to move about some, making the cage rock and swing, which no doubt provided much of the tribe's "amusement". By the look and smell of it, he had been there some weeks.

"We caught this crazy using our hostel," Yod said. "He claimed to be a surgeon, so we're giving him a chance to carve his way out. We don't like fakes." He glanced at Neq.

"A surgeon?" Neqa asked. "We haven't—" She stopped, remembering her guise as a nomad woman. But it told Neq that this man was not a crazy, for she would have known of him. Perhaps he deserved his punishment.

The prisoner looked dully at them. He was a small man with graying hair, very old by nomad definition.

"He says he's literate!" Yod said, laughing. "Show our guests your writing, Dick." In an aside to Neq: "All crazies have funny names."

The man reached around and found a tattered piece of cardboard, probably salvaged from one of the rifled crates the trucks had carried. He held this up. There were lines on it that did resemble the crazy writing of Neqa's recent report.

"Mean anything to you?" Yod asked Neq.

"No."

"Because you can't read—or he can't write?"

"I can't read. I don't know about him. Maybe he can't write either."

"Maybe. We could use a literate man. Some crazy books we found, don't know what's in 'em. Maybe something good."

"Why not test them on the crazy in the cage?" Neq asked.

"He lied about being a surgeon. We brought him a wounded man and gave him a dagger and he wouldn't operate. Said it wasn't clean, or something. Lot of excuses. So he'd lie about the books, too. He could tell us anything—and how would we know the difference?"

Neq shrugged. "I can't help you." He knew Neqa could, but he had no intention of giving her away.

"You're still Neq the Sword?"

"I always was."

"Prove it and you can join my tribe. We'll have to take your girl away, of course, but you'll get your turn at her."

"The man who touches her is dead," Neq said, putting his hand to his sword.

Yod laughed. "Well spoken. You have your part down well—and you shall have your chance to enforce it. Here is the circle." He glanced around and made a sweeping signal with his hand. Ready for this summons, the men of the tribe gathered.

In the temporary confusion, Neqa touched his hand. "That man in the cage—he *is* literate," she murmured. "He's from Helicon—a survivor. He may not be their surgeon—they had the best surgeon in all the crazy demesnes—but he's worth questioning."

Neq considered. If there were Helicon survivors. . . . "When I fight, you cut him down. I'll put on a show to distract them. You take him to the truck and get out. Use your knife; this bunch is rough. I'll find you later."

"But how will you—"

"I can handle myself. I want you out of here before it starts." He brought her to him suddenly and kissed her.

64

Stolen this fleetingly, the kiss was very sweet. "I love you."

"I love you," she repeated. "Neq! I can say it now! I mean it! *I love you!*"

"Touching," Yod said, breaking it up. "Here is your first match, crazy."

Neq let her go and faced the circle. A large clubber was there flexing his muscles. Most clubbers were large, because of the weight of the weapon; by the same token, most were clumsy. Still, no one could ignore the smashing metal, that could bash sword and torso right out of the circle in one sweep. Bog the Club had been astonishing. . . .

Suddenly, incongruously, Neq remembered how Bog had been balked. Once by Sol of All Weapons, the greatest warrior of all time; once by the Weaponless, who had broken his neck and killed him by a leaping kick. But once between those two honest contests, by the man Neq had not been able to remember before. The Rope! Sos the Rope—the man Miss Smith had remembered. He had looped the cord about the club, surprising Bog (who was not bright) and disarming him. Then the man had talked Bog into joining forces for doubles combat. The story of that audacity was still going the rounds. The Rope had not been nearly the man Bog was, but he had known how to use his luck. With Bog on his side, he had torn up several regular doubles teams. Bog plus a two-year child would have been a winning team! The Rope had finally overrated himself so far as to challenge Sol himself, and Sol had sent him to the mountain.

He would have to tell Neqa that, when they were out of this. And ask her whether by any chance her Sos had carried a little bird on his shoulder. Not that any of it was important today.

"That's Nam the Club," Yod said. "He says he's going to diddle your crazy blonde right after he diddles *you*. Should be no threat at all to—the fourth sword of a hundred?"

Neq gave Neqa a parting squeeze on the arm and urged her toward the caged man. The cage was beyond the immediate circle of spectators, partially concealed by the tree it hung from. If all of them faced toward the circle, and if there were enough noise, she would be able to cut open the cage and free the surgeon. Neq would have to arrange his fights—he knew they would keep sending men against him until they tired of this sport—to attract the complete attention of the outlaws. All of them.

She moved away, and he walked slowly toward the painted circle, drawing his sword. He stepped inside without hesitation.

Nam roared and charged. Neq ducked sidewise, staying within the ring. The clubber, meeting no resistance, stumbled on out.

"One down," Neq said. "Not much of a diddler, I'd say—either kind." He wanted to insult both clubber and tribe, to make them angry and eager to see the stranger get beaten. He wanted nobody's attention to wander.

Nam roared again, and charged back into the circle. This was another direct proof of his outlaw status, for no true warrior would re-enter the circle after being thus ushered out of it. To leave the circle during combat was to lose the battle—by definition. That was one of the ways the circle code avoided unnecessary bloodshed.

Neq did not wish to appear too apt with his blade too soon. If they recognized his true skill immediately, the game would be over, for they would know that he was the man he claimed to be, and that none of them could hope to match him. Yod would play fair only so long as he was certain of winning.

So Neq sparred with the clubber, ducking his clumsy blows, pinking him harmlessly, dancing him about in the circle. Meanwhile Neqa was edging toward the cage, not facing it but making covert progress.

When it seemed to him that interest was beginning to flag, Neq skewered Nam with a seemingly inept thrust, very like the one he had made against Hig the Stick at the

66

outset of his career as a warrior. It looked like a lucky stab by a novice sworder—as intended.

"So you *can* fight," Yod remarked. "But not, I think, quite up to the measure of your name. Tif!"

A sworder stepped toward the circle as men dragged the bleeding, moaning clubber way. Neq could tell at a glance that Tif was a superior sworder. The ante had been raised. The outlaws watched with greater anticipation.

Neqa was now close to the cage.

It required less art to fence with Tif, for the man was quick and sure with his blade, making defensive measures mandatory, not optional. But he was no threat to Neq. They jockeyed around, blade meeting blade clangingly, keeping the tribe absorbed. Every nomad liked a good show, even an outlaw.

Then Tif drew back. "He's playing with me," Tif called to Yod. "He's a master. I can't touch—"

Neq put a red mouth across Tif's throat and the man spouted his life's blood and fell. But it was too late. The "secret" had been exposed.

Neqa was working at the cage.

"So you *are* Neq the Sword!" Yod exclaimed. "We can't trust you, then. You'd want the tribe for yourself."

"I disbanded a tribe ten times this size!" Neq said scornfully. "This is nothing to me, and you are nothing. But you called me a crazy—so fight me for your tribe!" That might be an easy way out: take over the tribe, reconstitute it along honest nomad lines, bring all the trucks back to Dr. Jones.

Yod made an obscene gesture. "I'm not that kind of a fool. We'll have to shoot you."

If they brought out the bows again, Neq would have little chance. "I'll take on any two of you pitiful cowards in the circle!" he cried.

Yod was quick to accept the opportunity to save some face. It was always better for a leader to dispose of his competition honorably, if at all feasible. Otherwise other

67

leaders would arise quickly to challenge him, suspecting his weakness.

"Jut! Mip!" Yod shouted.

A dagger and a staffer came up, but not with the same eagerness the first two warriors had shown. Neq knew why: they were aware that one of them would likely die, even if the other finished off the challenger. Two men could generally defeat one—but the one could generally pick his man and take him out, if life were not the supreme object. Also, the tribe was beginning to mull the possibility of new leadership. If Neq were a better sworder than Yod, he might improve the lot of the tribe. So a certain discretion in loyalties was developing. As Yod was surely aware.

This was a smart combination. The staff would block Neq's sword and defend the pair of them, while the dagger would slice out from under that cover with either hand.

But Neq, like all warriors of the former empire, had been well trained in doubles combat. His reflexes sifted through automatically and aligned on "partner incapacitated; staff and dagger opposed." Except that he had no wounded partner to protect. That made it easier.

Yes, he owed a debt now to that Sos he had known! The interminable practice against all doubles combinations had seemed a waste of effort, for singles combat was the normal rule. But Sos had said that a top warrior had to be prepared for every eventuality. How right he had been!

As he engaged the pair, he saw that Neqa was still working at the cage. She could not devote her full attention to it, because she had to appear innocent. But she would shortly have the prisoner free.

Neq made the battle look good. He concealed none of his skill now. He kept the dagger at bay with a steadily flashing blade, and beat the staffer back by nipping at his hands and slamming against the staff itself. The pair had not fought like this often; they got in each other's way at crucial moments. A duo could be less effective than either warrior singly, if they were not properly coordinated. He could take them; it was only a matter of time. And they knew it; they were desperate, but had no way out.

Meanwhile, the tribe was watching, pondering loyalties, gravitating toward the strongest candidate for leadership.

"The crazy's escaping!" Yod cried.

Heads whipped about. Neqa and Dick the Surgeon were running away from the open cage.

Neq's ploy had almost worked. But that one small hitch—the random glance back of one spectator, perhaps only because a fly was bothering him—or because he was desperate himself to break up a pattern that did not favor him—had undone it all.

Now there would be hell to pay.

CHAPTER SEVEN

"After them!" Yod screamed. "Don't kill the girl!"

Men lurched to their feet, drawing their assorted weapons. Now they had to follow the leader they knew, for there was an immediate crisis. Had Neqa and the cage-man escaped cleanly while Neq fought, so that it was obvious that there was no chance to recapture them, then the leadership of Yod the Sword would have been open to serious question. Then Neq might have killed him quickly, and assumed command of the tribe. All that had been nullified by this one bad break.

Neq leaped from the circle and charged the chief. He still had a chance: he could take Yod hostage and buy time, and perhaps bargain for his own release and that of the other two. Or kill Yod outright, leaving the tribe no choice.

But Yod was too canny for that maneuver. Yod met him with drawn sword, yelling constantly to his men, stiffening their wavering loyalty.

Suddenly Neq was surrounded again. The warriors did not approach the battling sworders too closely, for he could still catch Yod in a desperation lunge; but that circle of weapons did prevent his escape. There were drawn bows—but again, he and Yod were moving so swiftly and the pack of other men was so great that the archers dared not fire until forced.

"The gun!" Yod yelled.

Then Neq despaired. He knew what a gun was. Tyl's tribe had returned from the mountain with guns and grenades and demonstrated them on targets. Guns had been employed against the underworld, and without them the assault would have been impossible. They were metal tubes that expelled metal fragments with great speed and force. The effect was similar to that of an arrow—but the gun could shoot farther and quicker, and it required far less skill to use. A cripple could kill a master sworder, with a gun.

Tyl had later decided that guns were inimical to the nomad mode of existence, and had called all such weapons in and hidden them. But he lacked authority over the complete empire, and some few had been lost. . . .

If Yod's tribe had a gun, Neqa and the surgeon would not escape. A gun could penetrate the metal of a truck.

Neq made his desperation lunge, breaking through Yod's guard and wounding him in the thigh. But as Neq recovered his stroke there was a blast of noise. Something struck his own thigh, and not an arrow.

The gun had been fired at him.

First he was relieved: they were not using it on Neqa!

Then he realized that it meant his own doom. The gun could kill him, and he would never get back to Neqa, and she would have to make the return journey alone. Unless the surgeon could protect her. But that man had not even been able to protect himself from being caged!

70

"Yield!" Yod panted. "Yield—or we shoot you down now!"

There seemed to be no choice. This was not a bluff. They might kill him anyway if he yielded—but they certainly had the means to do so if he did not. If Neqa was going to get away at all, she had had time enough; he could not help her by fighting longer.

Neq threw down his sword and stood waiting.

"You're smart," Yod said, as men grabbed Neq by the arms. "You saved your life." He touched his leg gingerly. "And you proved who you are. No lesser man could have wounded me in fair combat."

That was an exaggeration. Yod was good, but a score of empire sworders could have taken him handily. But Neq didn't feel obliged to enrage the man by pointing that out. He was now dependent on Yod's mercy, and the more Yod felt like an honorable victor, the more honorably he would act.

"But you did make a lot of unnecessary trouble by not yielding sooner," Yod continued. "And we can't trust you. I have promised you life—but I will consider your punishment. Tie him, men."

This time the tribesmen sprang to obey. They tied him: arms behind his back, tight, and a hobble-rope on his ankles. They propped him up against a post with his arms hooked behind it while they attended to other things.

Neq's wound smarted increasingly. The puncture was small, but through the large muscle. The fragment had to be lodged inside somewhere. There was not much bleeding; a sword wound would have been far worse. Except that the blade would have exited cleanly, permitting better healing.

There was a clamor as the pursuit party returned. "We got her!" a man exclaimed.

Neq saw to his grief that it was true. Neqa was being hauled along between two men, her wraparound torn,

71

portions of her torso exposed. She did not seem to be injured, however.

"She had a knife. Stabbed Baf," another man said. "Real wild girl. But we didn't hurt her."

"The crazy got away," another said. "But who cares?"

Yod's wound, not serious, had been bound. He was probably in as much pain as Neq, but did not show it. He had to maintain his facade before his tribe. "So she freed the crazy and stabbed one of our men," he mused. "And her man messed us all up, pretending to be a crazy, and killed Tif." He looked calculatingly at Neq. "OK—we'll teach them both a real lesson."

Yod walked up to Neqa. While the men held her arms, he ripped away the remainder of her clothing, flinging pieces of cloth aside to the delight of the others. "Man, she's a beauty!"

Neq struggled with his bonds, but they were firm. Some of the outlaws, watching him, chuckled; they *wanted* him to struggle. As they would have wanted Yod to struggle, had things worked out otherwise.

"Han!" Yod cried.

A youthful dagger approached nervously. Neq judged him to be a novice, perhaps fourteen.

"You never had it with a woman, did you?" Yod demanded.

"No—no," Han said, not looking at Neqa's nakedness.

"Now's your time. Go to."

Han backed away. "I don't understand."

"This crazy doll with the smooth skin and the sweet breast—you got her first. Right now."

Han glanced at Neqa, then guiltily away again. "But she's—she has his bracelet!"

"Yeah. That's funny. Leave it on."

"But—"

"He's going to watch this. On his own band. That's his punishment. And some of hers."

Han's body was shaking. "That's not right. I can't do that."

Neq strained furiously, but only skinned his wrists on

72

the rope. "I'll kill any man who touches her!" he screamed.

Neqa stood with her eyes closed, still held by two men. She seemed to have withdrawn from the proceedings. Her body was fair and slender and wholly out of place amid this rough crowd. Neq saw the outlaws looking at her, licking their lips.

Yod laughed. "You'll kill us all then, crazy-lover. 'Cause every man here's going to touch her—right now, where you can see."

"No!" Han cried. He ran at Yod.

Yod smashed him down backhanded. "You missed your chance, you sniveling kid. Now it's my turn."

Han stumbled back, bleeding from the lip, and fell near Neq. One of his daggers skidded on the ground.

Yod opened his pantaloons. The outlaws laughed. Neqa opened her eyes, struggled silently, and kicked her feet.

"Hold her legs too," Yod said. Two more men jumped forward to grasp her thighs.

Neq jabbed Han with his bound legs. When the youth turned dazedly toward him, Neq nodded toward the knife just out of his reach.

Han looked at the struggle going on as four men held Neqa by the hands and feet, spread-eagling her on the ground. Then he swept the blade toward Neq. It was still out of reach, for Neq could not pick it up.

Now Neqa screamed. Neq did not look. He had to get that knife immediately. He arched his body against the post, sliding his shoulders up, until his arms unhooked over the top of it. He fell over to the side, rolled, grabbed. The blade of the dagger sliced his hand, but he had it.

No one noticed. They were all intent on the show Yod was putting on.

Neqa screamed again, piercingly, as Yod's body covered her. She writhed on the ground and one of her hands slipped loose, but Yod stayed with her, grunting. The men grinned as they held her legs apart.

Neq twisted the knife, but he could not get it angled properly at the cord. His hands became slippery with his own blood. Then the strands began parting, reluctantly, as the flat of the blade wedged against them.

It seemed to take forever for the rope to give.

The outlaw chief stood up, short of breath. Neqa was sobbing brokenly.

"Hey—she was a virgin!" Yod exclaimed. "Look at that!"

The men crowded close to look. Neq, numbed to physical pain, sawed at the infernal rope.

"Why'd she have his bracelet, then?" someone demanded.

"I *heard* he wasn't much of a man outside the circle!"

Still the bands held. Han the dagger got up and fled, looking sick.

"All right—line up and take your turn," Yod said. "Every man of you. She's a good one."

The men lined up. Neqa had stopped crying. Three men still held her supine and spread on the ground.

Three more completed their business before Neq's hands finally were free. He severed the hobble-cord and lurched to his feet. He plunged the blade into the back of the fourth man as he lay astride Neqa. One down—four to go.

"Hey! He's loose!"

They piled on him. Neq fought savagely, but the dagger was not his weapon and he was grossly outnumbered. In moments they had him prisoner again.

Helpless, he had to watch while forty-four more men ravished his wife.

But it was not over.

"That's another he killed—and several more wounded," Yod said angrily.

"Kill him!" several cried.

"No. I granted him life. I want this bastard to suffer." Yod considered. "Cut off his hands." He lifted his sword.

Neqa, momentarily forgotten, climbed slowly to her

74

feet. Her eyes were staring. The dagger Neq had used lay near her on the ground. She stooped to pick it up.

Then, silently, she launched herself at Yod. Her blade sliced down the side of his face, catching part of one eye and eyeball.

Yod whirled, swinging his sword in an automatic reaction. It caught her across the neck, sinking in.

"Damn!" Yod cried, not seeming to realize the extent of his own wound. "I didn't mean to kill her! We *need* women!"

Neqa dropped to the ground, her blood spouting. Neq heaved his captors forward and they all fell.

It was too late for Neqa. Her teeth were bared in the rictus of the terminal agony; her red blood pooled in the dry dirt.

"Damn!" Yod repeated. "It's *his* fault! Hold him!"

They held Neq. Under Yod's grim direction they tied his hands again by the wrists, this time stretched forward. Four men hauled against his body while two pulled each rope, putting a terrible strain on his arms.

Yod positioned himself and swung his sword as though he were splitting wood.

Neq felt horrendous pain, and blanked out.

He came to immediately, or so it seemed. The pain had intensified unbearably, and sweet smoke stung his nostrils. They were holding torches to his wrists, burning them so that the flesh bubbled and popped.

Then nothing more.

CHAPTER EIGHT

He woke at dusk. His arms terminated in great crude bandages, hurting ferociously. Neqa lay beside him, pale and cold. His bracelet was still on her wrist.

He woke again, shivering, in the dark. Nothing had changed but the hour.

Toward morning he became delirious.

Light again, and someone was tending him. It was the cage-man, the surgeon. "You'll live. I'll bury her. You two saved me; I owe you that much."

"*I'll* bury her!" Neq cried weakly. But he had no hands.

He cursed meaninglessly as he watched Dick do it, as the dirt fell over her dead lovely face, over his bracelet, over his dreams. He had loved a crazy.

Miss Smith was gone forever. Neqa was dead.

Time passed. Dick the surgeon turned out to be no phony; he knew his medicine. The fevers and the chills subsided, strength of a sort came back; the thigh wound, excavated and cleaned, healed. But the hands were gone, and so was love.

Dick did everything, though he was no nomad. "I owe it to you," he said. "Her life, your hands—all because of me."

"They would have done it anyway," Neq said, not caring how the blame was parceled out. "They ambushed us before we ever saw you. We were already prisoners."

"She took several minutes to get me out of that cage, and she waited while I got some circulation back into my legs so I could walk. She would have gotten away, otherwise."

"You can't bring her back. If you owe me a favor, kill me too. Then I won't hurt any more—any way."

"I deal in life, not death. After Helicon, this is just an incident. I do owe you, but not that." He looked about. "We should get away from here. They dumped you both and left—but they could come back at any time. I was lucky they didn't see me following them."

Neq was not in a position to argue further. He talked with only a part of his consciousness, the least important part. The rest was obsessed with what had happened, and his impotence in the face of such calamity.

Only one thing kept him going. At first it was intangible, nebulous, a background emotion that gave him strength without comprehension. But gradually, as the days passed, it became solid, better defined, until it occupied the clear forefront of his mind, and he knew the need for what it was.

Vengeance.

"You are a surgeon," Neq said. "From what was mooted, the best in the world."

"Not necessarily. I was trained by a master, and he trained others. I've heard of remarkable surgery in the Aleutians—"

"You *do* talk like a crazy. Can you operate on me?"

"Without my equipment, my laboratory, drugs, competent assistants—"

"Was that what you told Yod?"

"Essentially. Surgery without sterilization procedures, anesthetics—"

"They sterilized my wrists, all right. With living torches!"

"I know. Yod is an outlaw, but he keeps his word. He wanted you to live."

"I keep my word too," Neq said. "But if there *are* ways to sterilize, why couldn't you—"

"Try a flaming torch on abdominal surgery!"

Neq nodded. "So Yod figured you were lying."

"I wasn't going to help him anyway. Any life I might save for him would mean death for others. His tribe deserves extermination."

"That may come," Neq said, but decided against clarifying the matter. "We'll get equipment, somewhere."

"Yes, with the necessary facilities I could operate. But in what manner? I can't give you back your hands. No one can do that."

"Tyl said—he said that the Nameless One, our Master of Empire, the Weaponless—by whatever name you know him—he said that man had been made strong by an underworld surgeon. You?"

"I had considerable assistance. And there was a strong

77

possibility of failure. As it was, I understand I rendered him sterile."

"If you could do that for him, you can do this for me."

"What do you want?"

Neq held up his truncated right arm. "My sword."

"Without a hand?"

"My sword will be my hand."

Dick studied him appraisingly. "Yes, I could do that. Insert a metal brace, attach the blade—it wouldn't be flexible, but there'd be plenty of power."

Neq nodded.

"It would be awkward," Dick continued, considering it further. "For sleeping, for eating. You would not be able to use that hand for any constructive purpose, except chopping firewood. But once you learned to control it you might reenter the circle. Much of your fighting skill is in your brain, I'm sure; you could overcome a substantial flexibility handicap. You would not be the warrior you were, but you could still be more than most."

Neq nodded again.

"I could give you a hook on the other arm, maybe even pincers. So you could dress, feed yourself."

"Start now."

"But I told you: I'll need anesthetics, instruments, sterilization—"

"Knock me out. Pass your knife through the fire."

Dick laughed without humor. "Impossible!" Then: "You're serious."

"Every day she lies cold while her murderers live is a torture to me. I must have my sword."

"But only Yod killed her, actually."

"They're all guilty. Every man who touched her—every one shall die."

Dick shook his head. "I'm afraid of you. I thought I had learned complete hatred during my time in the cage, choking on the miasma of my own refuse, but I fear what you will do."

"You won't have to watch."

"I'll be responsible, though."

"If you will not do it, tell me you will. Then kill me in my sleep."

Dick shuddered. "No, I'll fix you up. In my own way. We'll have to go back to what remains of Helicon for my supplies. They aren't all gone. I went back once to make sure. Gruesome experience."

"I know. But such a trip would take time!"

Dick looked at him. "You may dismiss pain when you're fighting in the circle or elsewhere. But this, when you're calm—let me make a small demonstration. Hold out your arm."

Neq held out one bandaged stump.

Dick took hold of it and applied pressure.

The pain started slowly, but built up appallingly. Neq took it, not flinching, knowing he was being tested but not knowing how long he could withstand it.

"That's just hand pressure," Dick said. "How will you like it when I start cutting? Scraping off the new scar tissue, cauterizing living flesh, laying open the muscle and tendons and tying wires to them? Hammering a metal spike into the radius—the long bone of the fore-arm? And another into the ulna, so that you will be able to twist your weapon as you once twisted your wrist, and perhaps to flex it a little. You're fortunate that your hands were severed below the wrists, leaving the main bones connected; that gives us much more leeway for reconstruction. But the pain—" As he talked, he twisted.

"Knock me out!" Neq cried again.

"I can't knock you out for the duration. I'd be substituting brain damage for hand damage. And I'll need your cooperation, because I'll be working without assistants. You have to be conscious. That means a local anesthetic—and even so, it will hurt a fair amount. Like this."

Neq, sweating acceded. He had not known there could be so much pain remaining in his mutilated limbs. "We'll go to Helicon."

"One other thing," Dick said. "I don't want to exploit your weakness by bartering with you now, not on a matter like this, but I have my own welfare to look out for. Once you have your sword, you won't need me or want me along."

"That's true."

"I'm not strong. I spent weeks, months in that cage. I lost track. I was able to exercise some, and I knew which muscles to concentrate on, but I never was strong for the wilderness life. I'm in no condition to survive by myself. I'd only get captured again, or killed by savages."

"Yes."

"Deliver me to the crazies before you start your mission."

"But that would take months!"

"Steal one of Yod's trucks. You can kill some outlaws in the process. I can drive; I can teach you—even with metal instead of hands. That's worth knowing."

"Yes . . ." Neq said, realizing that the man had a point. Dick had repaid anything he owed for his freedom by tending to Neq after the amputation and finding food— probably stolen from Yod's tribe at great risk—for otherwise Neq would have died. The operation was a new obligation. So it was a fair bargain.

And Neq *could* do some damage while taking the truck. Then the tribe would be on guard—pointlessly— while the two made their journey to the crazies.

It was, on balance, worthwhile.

Dick had a different entrance to Helicon. It was a stairway under a nomad burial marker, leading into a dank tunnel that in turn led to the main vault. Neq speculated privately that there must be numerous such ports— perhaps one for every underworld inmate of rank. That meant that many more could have escaped the flames and slaughter. No wonder the defense of the mountain had collapsed so quickly!

They fetched the drugs and instruments. Under the

film of ash much of Helicon was untouched. Had the underworlders had any spunk they could have restored it to a considerable extent. Nomads would have.

Neq could not do much, but he could carry. Dick fixed a pack for him and he hauled everything they needed to the nearby hostel and set up for the operation.

Time passed.

When Neq emerged from the intermittent haze of drugs and pain, his right arm terminated in a fixed full-length sword. His left had dull pincers that he could open and close with some discomfort by flexing wrong-seeming muscles.

The first time he tried to practice with the sword, the pain was prohibitive. But as his flesh healed around the metal and callus and scar-tissue formed, that problem eased. Eventually he was able to strike quite hefty blows without wincing.

His swordsmanship was hardly clever. Deprived of a real wrist, he had to maneuver mainly from shoulder and elbow. But he had power, for there was nothing to break or loosen. Skill would come with practice, for his mind had all the talent it had ever possessed.

He had to work with the pincers, too, flexing them each day, gaining proficiency. They were actually quite mobile when under proper control, and would lock onto an object or a knob like pliers, enabling him to pick up and squeeze without destroying. They, too, had great power.

Neq and Dick returned to Yod's territory to stalk a truck. There was a guard: Neq cut him down with an axe-motion swing of his sword, almost severing the man's head from his body. One more down. . . .

"Find a good one," he told the surgeon. "Load plenty of fuel. I'll watch for intruders."

"OK," Dick said, relieved. Neq knew the man did not like the killing, much as he hated the men who had tortured him. With Dick, hate was general, not subject to specific implementation; with Neq it was otherwise.

81

When he was alone, Neq hauled the body about with his clumsy pincers. He wanted to sever the penis that had violated Neqa, but he realized this would be meaningless. What he needed was a true token of his vengeance. That every man of the tribe would comprehend.

He struck down with his sword-arm, chopping at the gory neck. He struck again, and the head came loose.

He left it on the ground for a moment and walked to a sapling. He cut it down with one sweep, then caught the shaft in his pincers and held it for stripping. Finally he carved crude points on each end of the pole.

He returned to the loose head. He braced one foot on it and jammed with the pole. After several attempts he got the point wedged firmly inside the neck. He lifted the head, bracing the pole with both pincers and sword, and tried to set it upright in the ground.

It wouldn't go. Angry, and aware that he was wasting time dangerously, he jammed his sword down, making a cavity in the soil. He dropped the end of the pole in this and twisted it firm. It stood crookedly, but well enough.

Neq's monument was complete: the staring, dirt-smirched head of one of the men who had raped his wife. Mounted on a pole.

He had killed one of the men in the act, with the dagger, so this was the second. Of the forty-nine he had counted . . . Forty-seven to go.

If the tribe heard the truck take off, it was too late. No pursuit developed. If only they had been this lax before, Neq thought bitterly, he and Neqa would never have been caught. . . .

Dick had done well. Not only was there spare gasoline, there were blankets and tools and food. Apparently Yod used the trucks for supply storage, and had kept them in running condition. That was good management, for few nomads had knowledge of trucks.

The journey back was routine. There were roadblocks, but none by a major tribe, and Neq had little trouble discouraging them. In fact it was excellent practice for his stiff arm and sword.

He learned to drive, passing his sword through the wheel and using it to steer. His left extremity and his feet did the rest of the handling.

He delivered Dick to Dr. Jones, and trusted the underworlder to make the report Neqa had intended. Had his luck reversed all the way, this would have been the original truck, with her notes in the dash—but it was not. At least Dick himself had been there at Helicon for virtually all of it, so the report would be complete.

Then he turned back, driving the truck alone. His mission awaited him. Forty-seven lives. . . .

Vengeance.

CHAPTER NINE

Yod's camp was on guard day and night. It had been alert the whole time Neq had been absent. Ever since that first spiked head.

Good. He wanted them to suffer, just as they had wanted *him* to suffer. They had succeeded in torturing him . . . and now he would repay them in equal measure. He wanted every man to remember what the tribe had done, that day Neqa died, and to know that the time of reckoning was at hand. To know that every man of Yod's tribe would be staring on a pike.

First he took the guards—one each night, until they began to march double, and after that two each night. When they marched in fours he desisted; that was too chancy. He didn't care about himself, but he didn't want to die or become further incapacitated before he had completed his vengeance.

He avoided the foursomes and moved instead into the camp, killing a warrior in his sleep and taking the head. After that there were men on guard everywhere—one sleeping, one busy with chores, the third watching. The tribe was down to forty, and it was terrified.

Neq made no killings for a week, letting them wear themselves out with the harsh vigil. Then, when they relaxed, he struck again, twice. That brought them alert again.

They had to take the offensive. They swept the forest for him, trying to rid themselves of this stalking horror. He killed two more and left their heads for their fellow-searchers to find.

They went back to the perpetual alert, the men haggard. But they had to leave their immediate campsite to fetch water, to hunt, to forage. Three men, resting in the forest, gave way to fatigue and slept. They never woke.

Thirty-three remained.

There were fifteen women in the camp and twenty children. Now these noncombatants began standing guard over their men. Neq disliked this; he did not know what would happen to them once their men were gone. The women might be culpable for not encouraging some restraint in their men—no woman had shown herself during the whole of that nefarious day—but the children at least were innocent.

But he remembered Neqa, her piercing screams, her struggle as Yod raped her, and her failure to cry thereafter. His heart hardened. How often had this sort of thing happened before, with the women and children knowing and doing nothing? A person of any age who would not speak against such obvious wrong deserved no sympathy when the consequence of that wrong came back to strike him personally.

Three men came after him, guided by a dog. A clubber and two daggers. They must have borrowed the canine from some other tribe, for there had been no animals at the camp before. Neq had known it would come to this:

small cruising parties tracking him down relentlessly. He was ready.

He looped about, confusing the scent-trail, then attacked from behind. He killed one dagger before they could react, and swung on the other.

"Wait!" the man cried. "We—"

Neq's sword-arm transfixed his throat, silencing him forever. But as the blade penetrated, Neq realized he had made a mistake. He recognized this youth.

Han the Dagger.

The boy who had balked at raping Neqa. Who had helped free Neq, however temporarily. Who had fled while the sexual orgy continued, after trying to stop it.

"Wait!" the third man, the clubber, cried, and this time Neq withheld his stroke. "We did not do it. See, I am scarred. Where you struck me when we fought in the circle, and I—"

Now Neq recognized him too. "Nam the Club—the first of Yod's men I engaged," he said. "I tagged you in the gut." Nam might be better now, but he could not have participated then; not when that wound was fresh.

"The other dagger," Nam said, pointing to the first dead of this trio. "Jut—you fought him and Mip the Staff together. You did not wound them, but Jut hid. He knew what was coming. He never—"

Neq reflected, and realized that Jut's face was not among those he had seen at the raping. He had just killed two innocent men.

Not quite. Jut had not raped, but he had not protested either. He had fled, letting it go on. Even Han had had more courage than that.

"There were fifty-two men in Yod's tribe—plus Yod himself," Neq said. "Fifty-three altogether. Forty-nine did it, after hearing my oath. If you three did not, that accounts for fifty-two. What other man is innocent?"

"Tif," Nam said. "Tif the Sword. You killed him in the circle before—"

"So I did." Neq hesitated, feeling sick as he looked

down at Han. "Tif I do not regret, for it was a fair combat. Jut I might have spared, had I realized. But Han helped me, and—" Here regret choked off his words.

"That's why we came to you," Nam said. "We knew you did not have cause against us. We thought—"

"You turned traitor to your tribe?"

"No! We came to plead *for* our tribe!"

Neq studied him. "You, Nam the Club. You bragged of diddling. Had you been fit, would you have raped my wife?"

The man began to shake. "I—"

Neq lifted the tip of his sword. Blood dripped from it.

"I am a clumsy warrior," Nam said with difficulty. "But never a liar. And I am loyal to my leader."

Answer enough. "Were you friend to Han the Dagger?"

"No more than any other man. He was a stripling, softhearted."

Yes, the clubber was no liar. "I spare you," Neq said. "For the sake of this lad who was innocent and whom I wrongly slew. With choice, I would have cut you down instead, but now I spare you. But take this message to Yod: I spare no other."

"Then kill me now," Nam said simply. "Yod is a good leader. He is a rough man to resist, and he has bad ways about him, so that when he tells us to do something— even something like that—we must do it or suffer harshly. But he takes care of his tribe. He had to make an example."

"Not with my wife!"

"Discipline. He had to show—"

Neq's sword sliced off his nose and part of his talking mouth.

Then, sorry, Neq killed him cleanly.

And vomited, just as though he were a lad of fourteen again, at his first blooding.

At last he buried the bodies in honorable nomad

fashion, digging the grave and forming the cairn with his sword. He did not mount their heads.

Twenty-five remained, and they were dying more readily now. But Neq performed his ritual with a sense of futility. He knew that vengeance would not bring Neqa back or right the wrong he had done the nonraping tribesmen. Han the Dagger—there was no justifying that murder. Already Neq was guilty of acts as bad as those perpetrated against him—but he could not stop.

The second party to find him was female. Neq had learned caution, and did not attack them: five young women. He stood his ground and parlayed.

They were hauling a wagon covered by a tarpaulin. Neq watched it, judging that it was large enough to hold a man. A man with a gun. Neq stood in such a way as to keep one of the girls between himself and the wagon.

"Neq the Sword," their leader said. "Our tribe wronged you. But we offer atonement. Take one of us to replace your wife."

Surprised, he studied them more closely. All five were pretty—evidently the pick of the tribe.

"I have no quarrel with the women," he said. "Except that you did not protest the dishonoring of one of your kind. But I can not trust you and do not want you. Your men must die."

"It was our leader who was responsible," the woman replied. "Our men were bound to do Yod's bidding, or to die cruelly. Kill Yod and you have vengeance."

"I will kill him last," Neq said in fury. "He must suffer as he has made me suffer, and even then it will not be enough. Neqa was worth more than your entire tribe."

She seemed nonplussed for a moment, but made a decision. "We have brought him to you," she said. She gestured, and the other four approached the wagon.

Neq grabbed the leader with his left arm, his pincers threatening near her face, and held her before him as a shield against Yod's gun. She did not resist. Her sleek buttocks touched him.

The cover came up. The man inside was exposed.

It was Yod. But the man had no gun. He was dead, his hands severed, the hilt and blade of a dagger protruding from his mouth, and soaking in his own blood.

"Our men were bonded to him, and afraid," the captive woman said. "But *we* were not. We have brought your vengeance to you. Only spare the rest, for our children will perish if we are left without men."

"This is not vengeance," Neq said, troubled. "You have denied me my vengeance."

"Then kill us too, for we five killed Yod. Only leave this place."

Neq considered killing them, as she suggested, for they were trying to buy the reprieve of the guilty. But he found himself sick of it all. Now both Neqa and vengeance had been taken from him. What else was left?

He turned loose the woman. She merely stood, awaiting his response, and the others stood too, like waking dead. They were all young and fair, but there were pockets under their eyes and tension lines about their mouths, and they were less buxom than they might have been. Their vigil and their act of murder had scarred them already.

Neq lifted his sword and touched it to the leader's bosom. She blanched but managed not to flinch. He slid the blade along her front so that it cut open her dress of availability and the handmade halter beneath it, exposing her breasts and letting them droop. Yet they were full and handsome.

He had only intended to check her for weapons. If she had a knife on her person he would know for whom it had been intended, and that would justify what he might do. But there was no knife. Those breasts reminded him forcefully of Neqa's breasts . . . and suddenly he just wanted to forget.

Vengeance was too complicated.

He pushed her away and fled.

CHAPTER TEN

When Neq next took stock of himself, three years had passed. He was a scarred veteran of 28, still deadly in combat at an age when injury or death had retired many warriors. He had killed more men than any nomad he knew of—most of them outside the circle, for the circle code was virtually dead.

Abruptly he realized three things—or perhaps it was these things that had brought him to this sudden awareness. First, he was now the age Neqa had been when he knew her. Second, he was no closer to true vengeance than ever. Third, the true culprit had not been Yod and Yod's tribe, but the situation that had brought about the dissolution of the circle code. In the old days no woman had been molested, and no man had been required to fight unless he chose.

It came to him that his only true vengeance had to be constructive. Killing gained him nothing. What he had to abolish was not the *men* who had injured him, but the *system*.

That meant that Helicon had to be rebuilt.

Perhaps he had been working it out subconsciously the whole time. A concept of this complexity could not have struck him full-blown. But suddenly he had a mission, and the hurt that was the memory of Neqa abated, and the blood on his sword-arm assumed a certain vindication. He had no further desire to kill, for he had plumbed the depths of that and found it futile. He had no need to impress women, for there had been only one for him. He required no tribe, no empire, for he had long since experienced the heights of power and tired of them. He had his mission, and that was enough.

Rebuild Helicon, and the circle code could be restored. There would be supplies for the crazies, who would restock the hostels and subtly enforce their usual requirements, and the nomads would find themselves conforming, and the world he had known would come back. Slowly, perhaps; it might take decades. But it would surely come. And when the circle code lived again, outlaws like Yod would have no chance. Women would pass freely from hostel to hostel and from bracelet to bracelet, never forced, never hurt. The circle code was civilization, and Helicon was the ultimate enforcement of that code.

First he marched to the ruins of the mountain. He entered by Dick the Surgeon's passage and cleaned out the bones and the ashes. He reconstructed the damaged exits as well as he could and resealed the premises against intrusion and made the entire labyrinth bare but theoretically habitable. He worked slowly and carefully, pausing to feed himself when the need came and to search out supplies. A surprising amount had *not* burned. Perhaps the fire had suffocated soon after the people. Under layers of ashes the majority of Helicon's furnishings remained salvageable.

Neq sought no help, though his metal extremities were inefficient for this type of work and greatly extended the time that would normally have been required. It was tedious shoving a mass of cloth across interminable floors with his sword, mopping up the grisly grime, and his pincers were poor for setting hinges in new doors. But this was the place he had shared with Neqa, however briefly and horribly, and Helicon was somehow suffused by her presence, and blessed by it.

When he was done, a year had passed.

Then he went to see the crazies.

The minor crazy outposts had all long since been devastated, but the fortress-like administration building of Dr. Jones remained intact. And the old crazy chief was there, much the same as ever. He seemed never to have been young, and he did not age.

But there was now no girl at the front desk.

"How have you survived, with no defense?" Neq demanded. "It has been four years since I was here, and they have not been kind years. By the sword men live. But no man challenged me as I entered here. Anyone could ravage this place."

Jones smiled. "Would a guard have prevented you from entering?" When Neq merely glanced at his weapon, he continued: "I am tempted to inform you that our philosophy of pacifism prevailed . . . but that would not be entirely accurate. We hoped that the diminished services we offered would dissuade the tribesmen from violence, but there always seemed to be another more savage tribe on the horizon whose members were immune to reason. Our organization has been devastated many times."

"But you live unchanged!"

"Only superficially, Neq. My position remains tenuous." Dr. Jones began unbuttoning his funny vest.

The old crazy must have hidden when the outlaws invaded, Neq thought, and emerged to rebuild after the region was clear again. Tribes would not stay here long, for there would be little food, and the building itself was alien to the nomad way. Still, Dr. Jones must have courage and capability that did not show on the surface.

The crazy had finally finished with his buttons. He opened his vest and began on the clean white shirt beneath.

"How did you know me?" Neq inquired, hoping the man wasn't senile.

"We have met before, you remember. You took Miss Smith and released Dr. Abraham—"

"Who?"

"The Helicon Surgeon. He has been of immense assistance to us. Do you recognize his handiwork?" He opened his shirt to reveal his bony old chest.

Scars were there. It looked as though a dagger had cut him open, chopped up the ancient ribs, and made a careless foray into the meager gut. But somehow everything had been put together again, and what should have been a fatal wound had healed.

"Dick the Surgeon," Neq said. "Yes, he worked on me too." But did not raise his sword to demonstrate the surgery, afraid the gesture would be mistaken.

"I think it safe to assume I would have perished after that particular episode," Dr. Jones said, beginning the slow task of buttoning his shirt and vest. "But Dr. Abraham restored me. Since he would not have been present except for your timely assistance, I believe it is not farfetched to infer that I owe my preservation to you."

"For every life I may have saved," Neq said, "I have taken fifty."

Dr. Jones seemed not to have heard. "And of course his report enabled us to dispense with any further effort in the region of Helicon."

"Neqa died."

"Miss Smith . . . your bracelet . . ." Dr. Jones murmured, sifting through his information. "Yes, so Dr. Abraham informed us. He said the two of you were very close, and I am gratified to know that. She was a remarkable person, but alone." He did not say more, and Neq was sure the old crazy knew everything.

"I come to avenge her."

"Your reputation precedes you. But do you feel that more killing will satisfy your loss?"

"No!" And, with difficulty, Neq explained his conclusion about the real cause of Neqa's death, and his determination to rebuild Helicon.

Dr. Jones did not respond this time. He sat as if suffering from his venerable wound, eyes almost closed, breathing shallow.

Neq waited for several minutes, then raised his pincer-arm to touch the man and determine whether he was all right. Death by old age was something he had never encountered and was almost too horrible to contemplate. What were its symptoms?

Dr. Jones was alive, however. His eyes reopened.

"Do you require proof that I was there, in the mountain?" Neq asked. "I brought papers for you. I do not know what they say." He had saved out these singed writings because of Neqa's literacy; any writing reminded him of her.

Now the crazy reacted beautifully. "Papers from Helicon? I would be extremely interested! But I do not question your veracity. My thoughts were momentarily elsewhere."

Momentarily? Crazies were crazy, naturally!

Then Dr. Jones got up and left the room.

Neq remained, baffled.

A few minutes later Dr. Jones returned with another man, a rotund crazy in spectacles. "Please tell Dr. Abraham what you told me," Jones said. "About your plans."

It was Dick the Surgeon—the man Neqa had rescued from the cage! Now he only remotely resembled the thin fugitive of four years ago.

Neq repeated his philosophy and his plan.

"Why do you come to us?" Dick asked, as though he had never had experience with the wilderness.

"Because I am a sworder, not a builder. I can't read, I can't operate the machinery of Helicon. You crazies can."

"He knows his limitations," Dr. Jones observed.

"But he is a killer."

"Yes," Neq agreed. "But I have had enough of killing." He lifted his arm. "I would make this sword into—"

"A plowshare?" Dr. Jones asked.

Neq did not answer, not being familiar with the term.

"Your former leader, Robert of Helicon," Dr. Jones said to Dick. "Was he not a ruthless man?"

"Robert? Oh, you mean Bob. Yes, ruthless but efficient.

Maybe you're right." Dick looked at Neq. "It is ugly, but—"

Neq did not follow much of this. "I have cleaned and restored the mountain, but I cannot do more without your help. I can't fill it with people who can make it function. That is why I'm here."

"It would take a year for a man in your condition to tidy up that carnage!" Dick exclaimed.

"Yes."

There was a silence. The crazies hardly seemed enthusiastic!

Finally Dr. Jones brought out a sheet of paper. "Bring me these people," he said, handing it to Neq. "Those who have survived."

"I can not read. Is this the service you require of me in exchange for your help?"

"In a manner of speaking, yes. I must ask you to tell no one of your project. And I must advise you that your weapon will be valueless in this endeavor—perhaps even a liability."

That seemed to be the extent of his answer. Neq glanced at his sword, wondering whether he should remind the old crazy that it was impossible for him to set aside his weapon, useful or not. "Tell me the names."

"You can remember them accurately?"

"Yes."

Dr. Jones picked the paper out of Neq's pincer-grasp and read. "Sos the Rope. Tyl of Two Weapons. Jim the Gun."

Neq halted him, astonished. "Sos the Rope went to the mountain . . . oh, I see. He may be alive after all. Tyl is master of the largest remaining tribe. Jim the Gun—"

"You may know Sos better by his later designation: the Weaponless."

"The Weaponless! Master of Empire?" And yet of course it fit. Sos had gone to the mountain; the Weaponless had come out of it. To take the wife he had always

94

wanted—Sola. Neq should have made the connection long ago.

"Have you changed your mind?"

Angry, Neq kept silence while he considered. The crazies were trying to set him an impossible task! Was it to be certain he would fail? Was this really their way of refusing assistance? Or was Dr. Jones serious, having decided that it was necessary, before Helicon could be rebuilt, to eliminate its destroyers? The Weaponless, Tyl, Jim the Gun—these had been the architects of Helicon's demise. The Weaponless had provided the motive; Tyl the manpower; Jim the weapons. . . .

Perhaps it made sense. But how to locate the Weaponless now! If the man lived, so did the empire, and Neq himself still owed him fealty!

"I think the Weaponless is dead," Neq said at last.

"Then bring his wife."

"Or his child," Dick said.

"And if I bring these people to you, then you will give me the help I need for Helicon?"

"There are more names." Dr. Jones read them: all unfamiliar.

"I'll bring every one that lives!" Neq cried recklessly. *"Will you help me then?"*

Dr. Jones sighed. "I should be obliged to."

"I do not know where to find them all."

"I will travel with you," Dick the Surgeon said. "I know many of the Helicon refugees by sight, and have some notion where they might hide. But it would be your job to persuade them to come—without killing them."

Neq mused on this. The company of the surgeon did not appeal to him, but it did promise to facilitate an onerous task. "I can't tell them and I can't kill them. Yet I must make them come. The leading warriors of the old empire, including the very man who—" He shook his head. "All because I want to rebuild Helicon, and restore your source of supply, so that you can bring back the circle code."

Dr. Jones didn't seem to comprehend Neq's irony. "You have the essence, warrior."

Angry and disappointed, Neq walked out. But Dick the Surgeon followed.

CHAPTER ELEVEN

Tyl's tribe was not as large as it had been in the heyday of empire, for he had taken losses in the Helicon reduction and in the anarchy following. But its demesnes were larger because of the general decimation of nomads in recent years. Now it represented a kind of civilization itself, for shelters had been built, fields cultivated, weapons forged, and the circle code was enforced. There was now a preponderance of staffs, clubs and sticks, mostly wooden weapons, because metal was much cruder than Helicon's product. The fine old weapons were increasingly precious now. Neq knew that those who carried swords of the old type were veterans, for today a man was challenged as frequently for possession of a superior weapon as for woman or service or life.

"You come to challenge *me*?" Tyl demanded incredulously. "Have you forgotten the code of empire: the sub-chiefs of the Weaponless may not war against each other?"

"They may not war for mastery," Neq answered. "No, I have not forgotten. But the empire is dead, and so are its conventions."

"It is not dead until we know the Weaponless is dead —and he is a difficult man to kill, as you would know had you ever met him in the circle. And the circle code is not dead where my tribe travels."

"It is dead wherever your tribe departs, however." But

Neq approved the fine order Tyl maintained. "I did not say I came to challenge you with weapon, for I may not use my sword on this mission. Were any man to question my competence in the circle, I should be glad to show him my blade—but not for mastery, not for death, only for demonstration, no blood shed. I challenge you only to do a service for me, and perhaps for the nomad society."

Tyl smiled. "I would do you a service without inducement in the circle, however circumspectly hinted, for we were comrades in better days. And I would aid the nomad society if I only knew how. What is it you wish?"

"Go to the crazies."

Tyl laughed.

"Nevertheless," Neq said, remembering how Sol had reacted to disbelief, so many years ago. More than half Neq's life had passed since his conquest by Sol of All Weapons.

Tyl looked at him more closely, responsive to the tone. "I have heard—this is merely rumor—that you were injured in a conflict with outlaws."

"Many times."

"The first time. That they overcame you by means of the advantage of fifty men and a gun, and cut off your hands."

Neq glanced down at his cloth-wrapped extremities, nodding.

"And that you achieved some semblance of vengeance ... nevertheless."

"They slew my wife."

"And she was a crazy?"

"She was."

"Yet now you espouse another crazy cause?"

Neq's sword-arm twitched under the cloth. "Do you slight my wife?"

"By no means," Tyl said quickly. "I merely remark that you have had adventures I have not, and must have strong motive for your mission."

Neq shrugged.

97

"I will go to the crazies," Tyl said. "If I do not find reason to stay, I will return to my tribe."

"That suffices."

"Any other favor I can do you?" Tyl inquired dryly.

"If you can tell me where the Weaponless might be."

Tyl controlled his surprise. "He has been absent five years. I doubt he resides within the crazy demesnes."

"His wife, then."

"She remains my guest. I will take you to her."

"I thank you."

Tyl stood, a fair, rather handsome man, a leader. "Now that our business is done, come with me to the circle. I would show my men swordsmanship of the old style. No blood, no terms."

It was Neq's turn to smile. On such basis he could enter the circle. It had been long since he had sworded for fun, following the rules of empire.

And it was a pleasure. Whether Tyl remained his superior no one could say, for Neq's technique had necessarily changed, and they were not fighting in earnest. But Tyl's art was beautiful, rivaling that of Sol of All Weapons in the old days, and the display the two of them put on left the more recent members of the tribe gaping. Feint and counterfeint; thrust and parry; offense and defense, with the sunlight flashing, flashing, flashing from living blades and the melody of combat resounding to the welkin.

When they finished, panting, the tribesmen remained seated around the circle, rows and rings of armed men, silent. "I have told you of Sol," Tyl said to them. "And of Tor, of Neq. Now you have seen Neq, though his hands are gone. Such was our empire."

And Neq felt a glow he had not experienced in years, for Tyl was giving him public compliment. Suddenly he longed for the empire again, for the good things it had brought. And his determination to complete his mission despite the barriers the crazies were erecting was doubled.

* * *

Sola had aged. Neq remembered her as a rare beauty, truculent but gifted with phenomenal sex appeal, fit for a single man to dream about. Now her face was lined, her body bent. Her long dark hair no longer flowed, it straggled. It was hard to believe that she was only two or three years older than he.

"This is Neq the Sword," Tyl said to her, and departed.

"I would not have recognized you," Sola said. "You look old. Yet you are younger than I. Where is the shy young warrior with the magic sword and golden voice?"

To each his own perspective! "Does the Weaponless live?"

"I fear he does not. But he would not return to me, regardless."

Neq was surprised. "To whom, then?"

"His other wife. She of the underworld."

His interest intensified. "You know of Helicon?"

"I know my husband laid siege to the mountain, because she was there. She has his bracelet and his name."

"She lives?"

"I do not know. Do *any* live—who were there when the fire came?"

"Yes," he said. Then, quickly: "Or so it is rumored."

She was on the slip immediately. Sola had never been stupid; she had taught the warriors counting and figuring. "If any live, *she* lives. I know it. Seek her out, tell her I would meet her. Ask her—ask her if my child—"

Neq waited, but she only cried silently.

"You must go to the crazies," he said finally.

"Why not? I have nothing to live for."

"This woman of the Weaponless—what name does she bear?"

"His old name. Sos. The one I would have had, had I not been a foolish girl blinded by power. By the time he was mine, he was *not* mine, and he was nameless."

"So she would be Sosa. She would know if the Weaponless lives?"

"She is *with* him if he lives. But my child—ask her—"

Neq made a connection. "Your child by Sol? Who went with him to the mountain?"

"More or less," she answered.

He thought of the skeletons he had swept from the underground halls. A number had been small—children and babies. Yet there had been several exit passages such as the one Dick the Surgeon had used. There had been some unburned caverns as well as the little wagon-tunnels to scattered depots. Some adults had escaped, perhaps many; no one knew how large Helicon's population had been. Some children could have. . . .

"I have one more name for you," Sola said. "Var—Var the Stick."

Neq had some vague recollection of such a warrior, a helper to the Weaponless who had disappeared at the same time. "He will know where to find the Weapon-less?"

"He must know," she said fervently. "He was the protégé of my husband, and sterile like him.

Neq wondered how she could know such a thing. But he remembered the rumors about this woman, and how she had gone to Sos's tent in the badlands camp, and wondered again. "I will seek Sosa," he said. "And Var the Stick."

"*And* my child—Soli. She would be thirteen now, al-most fourteen. Dark-haired. And—" She hesitated. "You remember the way I used to be?"

"Yes." Her figure had stimulated him many times, fif-teen years ago.

"She favors me, I think."

Soli would be a beauty, then. Neq nodded. "I will send them all to the crazies—if they live."

"I will wait there." And for some reason she was cry-ing. Perhaps it was the weakness of an old woman who knew she would never see her husband or her daughter again; who knew that their bones lay charred and buried near the mountain of death.

* * *

100

Dick the Surgeon located several of the strangely-named fugitives in the next few months. Men like John and Charles and Robert, men old and feeble and obviously unused to the way of the nomads despite their recent years among them. Some were refugees from Helicon; others seemed to be crazies, cut off by the breakdown of civilization. Dick talked to them, and glimmers of hope brightened their forlorn faces and they agreed to come with Neq—to Neq's suppressed disgust. Now he had to forage for them, and guard them against outlaws, for they were almost unable to do for themselves and could not make the trek to Dr. Jones alone. A man with no hands taking care of men with no gumption!

But these creatures had survived because they had talents certain tribes wanted—literacy, hand skills, knowledge of guns. Most of the names on his list seemed not to have survived; no doubt they belonged to bones he had swept in Helicon.

When he could, he inquired about his other names: Var, Sosa, Soli. But there was no memory of these among the nomads—not since the destruction of Helicon.

Finally he brought his small group back to the crazy building. Almost a year had passed.

"You are still determined to rebuild Helicon?" Dr. Jones inquired.

"Yes." He did not add *in spite of you*.

"You did not locate all the persons listed."

"I have not finished. I merely deliver these to you, who could not deliver themselves. Many of the rest are dead. You saw Tyl and Sola?"

"They are here."

So Tyl had remained! What had the crazy said to him?

"I have not found the Weaponless—but now I search for his underground wife, Sosa, and for Sola's child, and for Var the Stick. These may help me to locate him—or his cairn."

"Interesting you should mention those names," Dr. Jones murmured. "You are illiterate, as I recall."

101

"I am a warrior."

"The two abilities—reading and fighting—are not necessarily mutually exclusive. Some warriors are literate. But you have no notion of the content of the papers you delivered to us?"

"None."

"Let me read some excerpts to you, then." And the old crazy brought a similar sheaf up from the bowels of his desk.

> AUGUST 4, B118—The siege has abated, but the mood is ominous. Bob has arranged some kind of contest of champions, but has as yet selected no man to represent Helicon. We are not geared for this nomad circle-combat; it is folly. We have in Sol the Nomad one of the most formidable primitive fighters of the age, but I know he will not take up weapon against his own kind. He hates it here; he really did come to die, and he resents what we did to him: making him live because we made his daughter live. Sosa has kept him pacified somehow; I don't know how that marvelous woman does it. Sol's daughter *is* his life.
>
> But I ramble too much about other people's business, as an old bookworm will. Surely I have concerns of my own: this premonition that this is the terminus, the extinction of the life we have known, and perhaps of civilization itself. . . .

"The mountain!" Neq exclaimed. "The siege of Helicon!"

"These notes are by Jim the Librarian—a literate and sensitive man."

"He is on my list! A man of the underworld!"

"Yes, of course. But it will not be necessary to look for him further."

"To rebuild!" Neq cried, comprehending what should have been obvious all along. "The men who *know*!"

"Certainly. Obviously nomads could not rebuild the foreign technology of Helicon unassisted, however noble their motives. But a nucleus of such survivors, together with the most capable nomads and, er, crazies, under a strong, sincere leader—it can be done, we suspect."

"That's why you want the Weaponless—to lead!"

Dr. Jones looked at him with compassion. "I hope you will not be disappointed that we do not deem you fit to lead the actual restoration. What you are attempting is noble, and you shall certainly receive due credit for your dedication and effort; but the complexities of technology and discipline—"

"No, you are right," Neq said with mixed emotions. He *was* disappointed, but also relieved. "I never thought to stay in Helicon myself. I saw the carnage—only crazies could *like* it there, away from the sun, the trees—" As he spoke he realized why Tyl had been on the list. They needed strong and competent leadership, and Tyl was that. He had been second in command to the Weaponless, and before that to Sol of All Weapons. He had as much experience in managing men as any nomad, and he was a top warrior who never let discipline slide. The underworld would be a kind of empire.

"I'm glad you understand. Training and temperament are paramount. In a pressure situation where swords and clubs are not the answer—"

"But the Weaponless—he *destroyed* Helicon! Why should he help it now?" Yet obviously Dr. Jones wasn't depending entirely on the Weaponless. He was grooming Tyl as an alternate.

"Sos the Weaponless was *of* Helicon. Dr. Abraham made him what he was, on the unfortunate directive of their leader." Dr. Jones cogitated for a moment. "Dr. Abraham was not aware of the politics leading to the disaster. He was sleeping when the fire started, and dazed when he escaped. He supposed the nomads had done it."

"Hadn't they?" Leading question!

"Not directly. Here is Jim's final entry."

AUGUST 8, B118—How can I express the horror I feel? Soli was my child too, in the sense that I taught her to read and I loved her as my own. Almost daily she came to the library, an absolutely charming little girl— indeed, I believe she divided her time almost evenly between my books and her father's weapons. Yet now—

I blame myself. She came to me in tears just three days ago with a story I refused to credit: that Bob intended to murder both Sol and Sosa, her Helicon parents, if she did not go on a dangerous mission *outside*. She had been sworn to secrecy, she claimed, lest they be slain regardless—but she had to tell someone, and I agreed to keep her confidence, thinking it a fantasy of a juvenile mind. I advised her that she had misunderstood, that Bob had the best interest of Helicon at heart, and had only meant that her parents' lives might be endangered, as we are all endangered, by this continuing nomad siege. I recommended that she agree to the secret mission, for surely (if it were not a product of her own lively imagination) it was merely a device to get her safely from the scene of action before another crisis occurred. 'We value our children most of all,' I informed her fatuously.

Now she is dead, and I deplore my hopeless naivete. Bob sent her to Mt. Muse, to engage in physical combat with the nomad champion, and of course the brute killed her. The nomads are celebrating; we can overhear their foul carousing. 'Var the Stick!' they cry—but I don't believe they realize that their precious barbarian champion, shielded from their view on the flattop mesa a dozen miles south of here—was pitted against *an eight year old girl*.

Confound the promise of secrecy I made! I have told Sosa what Soli told me. I had to, for Sosa is more the mother of that dear girl than her nomad dam could ever have been. Sosa would have learned of it soon enough, less sympathetically. I am sure she will relay it to Sol, and I do not speculate what will develop now. Were I a warrior-type in such a situation I am sure I would not be gentle. But I am only a futile old man.

I am taking poison.

104

There was a pause.

"Var the Stick—he was the nomad champion? He killed Sol's child?"

"So it would appear. If you were Sol—"

"I *am* a warrior-type! I would have put Var's head on a spike in the forest for all to see. And Bob's. And all others responsible. And—"

Dr. Jones steepled his hands in a way he had. "And . . .?"

"And accomplished nothing," Neq said slowly. "Vengeance is not the answer. It is only vengeance. Only more sorrow."

Dr. Jones nodded. "I believe you are in a position to comprehend Sol's motives, then and later. He was a thorough nomad, despite his residence in Helicon for those years. Would he have ignited the incendiary stores there?"

"I don't know about that," Neq said, not understanding one of the words. "But I think there was gasoline down there. And other stuff that would burn. I think he fired it all. In the name of vengeance. Those bodies were scorched!" And more than scorched.

"And later—would he have returned?"

"To view the destruction, after he knew it had accomplished nothing? No, he would not return. . . ."

"Yes. Yet if we were to rebuild Helicon, how could we be certain that such a thing would not happen again?"

"I do not know," Neq said honestly.

"Go and find out," Dr. Jones said.

"But you agreed to help if I brought you these people!"

"And we shall. But of what use is it to rebuild Helicon if it remains liable to destruction by the forces that brought it down before? The human forces."

Neq had no answer for that.

"Forget the remaining names on the list," Dr. Jones said kindly. "The nucleus is almost sufficient now. Look instead for Sol and Sosa and Var, should he somehow have survived Sol's quest for vengeance. Learn whether

105

Sos the Weaponless was more directly involved; perhaps his disappearance is relevant. Ascertain the truth—and suggest how we may prevent any conceivable recurrence. Only then will we be assured that our endeavor is secure."

CHAPTER TWELVE

The six year old spoor of both Var the Stick and Sosa had to begin at Helicon. The one had been with the nomads, the other with the underworld. Both had vanished in that final, devastating encounter. Probably both were dead—but then his quest for information was dead, too. Sol and the Weaponless had much better chances of survival—but neither would have been party to the heart of Helicon's failure: the inner workings of Bob's mind. For had Bob not sent an innocent child to her death, both he and Helicon might have weathered the siege. The underworld defenses were certainly formidable enough. Why had Bob, by all accounts a capable leader, erred so brutally and calamitously? Would the next leader err the same way? There was the key.

Helicon was as he had left it: tight and clean. He re-explored its several exits, pondering whether a woman might have used one to escape. Certainly she might! To this extent Sola's intuition must be correct: Sosa, with forewarning of Sol's intent, was the most likely of all the underworlders to have escaped cleanly. Sol could have been trapped in his own conflagration—and the Weaponless, outside, could well have entered Helicon in a desperate attempt to find Sosa . . . and failed, and died.

He scouted the exterior again, and made a trek to Mt. Muse, to see where a warrior might have gone after slaying a child. But he could not climb to the mesa—and anyway, Var had returned to the nomad camp to be feted for his barbarism. There was no answer there. Tyl himself had seen Var after the "combat of champions" but had only known that Var disappeared shortly thereafter, and then the Weaponless. Neither had given any advance hint of what was to happen. There had been no evidence of foul play.

There were outlaw tribesmen in this region. Some Neq and Dick had encountered before; no one had known of Var or Sosa. Of course there was considerable turnover here, for the outlaws warred constantly with one another in this land of no honor, and few lived long.

The locals were not eager to answer more questions. Neq's uncovered sword convinced them. Still he learned nothing.

He moved out, making great circles around Helicon, searching out men and tribes he had not met before. Many balked—but as the blood dripped from his sword, his questions were answered. Negatively. Only six years had passed, but many of these men did not know what he meant by "Helicon."

Months passed, his circles widened, and he accomplished nothing. But he would not stop. Instead he became more devious in his questioning. "Six years ago, perhaps seven—did a stranger pass through your territory? A lone sticker? A small woman? Someone masked or hidden or mysteriously wounded?

And finally he got a meaningful response, from an old warrior of the defunct empire, who had drifted to this region before the siege and remained, retired. "I saw a stranger then—a pale, slender man who spoke no word."

This did not sound like Var the Stick, who was a large, grotesquely mottled youth. "What was his weapon?"

"I did not see it. But he hauled a barrow with a staff protruding, and he reminded me of—"

"Of whom?" Neq prodded, remembering a man who had hauled a barrow.

"Of Sol of All Weapons. But that could not be, for Sol went to the mountain half a dozen years before."

So he had looked for Sosa, but found Sol! But that was

almost as good, for surely they had escaped Helicon together. His long search had been rewarded . . . perhaps.

Suddenly the trail was hot. There were passes where a man would normally travel, places where he might camp. Neq traced Sol's course, finding many who had seen the barrow-man pass. Some had challenged him to the circle, for that was before the effect of Helicon's fall had been felt in the nomad society and honor was strong, but the man had avoided all such contacts. No one Neq met claimed to have fought the barrow-man in the circle.

That proved they were speaking honestly. Sol had been the greatest circle warrior of all time, except for the artificially forged juggernaut of the Weaponless—and the battle between the two had been so even as to be merely chance in the decision. Sol might have lost his edge during six years in Helicon—but not much, if he were training his daughter regularly. Any man who brought Sol to combat against his preference must have paid the obvious penalty. Only those who had *failed* to fight him could have survived.

And why had Sol avoided encounters? Obvious, now: because he had more important business. He was going somewhere.

But not, it seemed, with Sosa. No one had seen her. Sol was traveling alone. Why should that be?

Neq knew. Sol was following the man who had killed his daughter. Var the Stick.

Vengeance.

A lone warrior would not have been remarkable. That's why Var himself hadn't been remembered. But the barrow—that stuck in many minds, because it was unusual. Because it brought to mind the one warrior everyone knew about. Now that Neq inquired about that specifically, the long faded memories returned.

Sol had departed Helicon and traveled northwest, detouring around badlands and avoiding established tribes. Why northwest? Because Var the Stick must have fled that way.

108

And he had! Neq picked up the memories now—the skin-mottled man, also no talker, deadly with the sticks . . . and his boy companion.

Boy companion?

And abruptly—the Weaponless. He was on this route too, incredibly. Was he following Var—or Sol? To protect the first from the second? What a battle of titans, if Sol and the Weaponless should meet again!

Yet none of them had returned. All the key figures had vanished, and not in the Helicon conflagration. Where had they gone?

And where had the boy come from—the boy with Var the Stick? Had he had a little brother? After months of finding too little, Neq had found too much!

He continued the chase doggedly. His hopes for the restoration of Helicon were somehow bound in with this mystery, and he would not stop without the answer. His cast of characters remained set: three men and a boy, not together, traveling northwest. The riddle of Helicon's demise . . . perhaps.

But the trail faded near the northern limit of the former crazy demesnes. Neq cast about for a month in the increasingly bitter winter, but the natives knew nothing. He had either to give up, or to leave the territory of the nomad society, as his quarry seemed to have done.

He hesitated to go farther north. His metal extremities were excellent for combat and simple hunting, for he had a bow he could brace on his sword and fire lefthanded with the pincers with fair accuracy. But against true wilderness and snow he was weak, and he knew that guns were more common in the northern realm. He could not use a gun himself, and had to be extremely wary in the presence of such a weapon.

And so he continued his futile search in the land of the nomads long after his real hope of success was gone.

One day Tyl of Two Weapons appeared, alone. "Are you ready for help?" Tyl inquired as if this were routine.

Neq's pride had suffered with the winter. "I welcome it," he said.

Tyl did not clarify the obvious: that word had reached him of Neq's futility. "I do not wish to bargain with a comrade of empire, but the crazy has laid his stricture on me as on you. My help is for a price."

Dr. Jones peculiar yet subtly forceful hand again! "What price?"

"I will name it when the occasion arises."

Neq knew Tyl for an honest man. "Accepted."

"We travel north?"

"Yes." With Tyl along, they could manage. The search could resume. "Sol of All Weapons. The Weaponless. Var the Stick. A boy. All went north, none returned. Find one of these, and we may learn why Helicon failed. Var might have learned the truth from Soli, before he killed her; Sol might have gotten it from Bob of Helicon, before he killed him. The Weaponless . . . may have his notions, for he negotiated with Bob about the combat of champions. The boy—I don't know."

Tyl considered. "Yes. The secret lies between Bob and Soli. Too bad neither survived. . . ." He trailed off, pondering something; but he did not amplify his thought.

Tyl had a gun, and was competent with it. Tyl had hands. Tyl had a way with strangers that Neq lacked. The trail reappeared.

And disappeared. They followed it to the northern ocean, where a forbidding tunnel went under, and there it stopped. "If they went in there," the natives opined, "they are gone forever. The machine-demon consumes intruders."

Tyl distrusted it for a more practical reason. "I saw strange things come from the tunnels as the mountain burned. Animals with tremendous eyes and mouths, that a sword would not stop. Rats with no eyes. Some of my men died after merely touching such creatures. Jim the Gun said they carried radiation kill-spirits; he heard them on his click-box. I would not enter such a place without an army, and then I would need good reason."

Neq agreed. He had seen strange corpses in the fringe passages beyond the burn-zone of Helicon, and many radiation markers, and at night he had heard the scamperings of things that could have been similar to those Tyl described. Had he not had strong motivation, he would never have completed the long chore of cleaning the underworld rooms and passages. It would be folly to brave this unfamiliar tunnel as anything but a last resort. Rumors of horror were often well-founded, these days.

So they quested north, along the coast—and the trail resumed! Two men, one grizzled and huge, the other pale and silent. No blotch-skinned sticker; no boy.

Then Tyl spied a nomad campsite. "See—they built a fire, here, and pitched some kind of tent here, with guides around it to lead off the water from rain. The locals don't do that; they stay in square houses."

"But this is recent. Five, six days, no more. It can not be our quarry."

"True. But what would nomads be doing here? We should question them."

"Question the locals. Some would have seen the nomads pass."

Tyl nodded thoughtfully. "Strange we have heard nothing of these before."

They questioned the locals, and learned that two nomads, a man and a woman, had passed through, traveling south.

"South?" Neq demanded. "Where did they come from?"

The people only shrugged, not knowing or caring what the barbarians did or which direction they went.

Sol and the Weaponless had gone north; these others were *from* the north. Their trails might have crossed.

They made a rapid excursion south again, tracing the strangers, following a course that skirted dangerously close to posted radiation zones. A large, gruff man and a

111

rather pretty woman who kept to themselves and made swift progress. Tyl would question native villagers—a village was a kind of stationary tribe, unique to this locale—while Neq scouted the countryside for further traces.

Neq looked up one such afternoon to discover a grotesque man watching him. Huge and shaggy, hunched-backed, with grossly gnarled hands curled about home-made singlesticks, and mottled skin showing under his heavy winter coverings—the man was more like a bad-lands beast than a nomad. But nomad he was, and he had already assumed a stance of combat. His long arms and heavy chest suggested enormous power; he would be savage with those sticks!

Mottled skin. . . .

"Var the Stick!" Neq cried, amazed.

The other spoke, but it sounded more like a growl. By concentrating, Neq made out the gist. "You followed me for days. Now give cause why I should not drive you off."

Neq unveiled his sword. "Cause enough here. But first you must answer my questions, for I have sought you long."

"A changeling!" Var rasped, seeing Neq's arms. "Do you know the circle?"

Neq was surprised. "You speak of the circle? *You*, slayer of children?"

"Never!" Var roared, coming at him. There was something wrong about his legs; though he wore boots, he did not walk like a man. A true beast in nomad outfit . . . it was no longer a mystery why he had killed the young girl Soli. He had probably eaten her.

Var struck at him and Neq parried, smiling grimly. He had no fear of hand-hewn weapons, and a clumsy charge was the simplest to terminate. But first he needed information.

Var was more artful than his appearance suggested. As Neq dodged aside, so did he, so that they met squarely. One stick shot toward Neq's face while the other blocked his sword. Var had met many a blade before!

So much the better. Neq's pincers also blocked defensively while his sword whistled. He struck first at the other's weapon, seeking to cut a stick in half. He preferred to disarm this monster gradually, lingeringly, not hurting him much . . . until after the truth was known.

"Before I down you," Var grunted, "Tell me your name."

"Neq the Sword." This courtesy of identification was due even for a beast.

Var fought for a while, quite skillfully, pondering behind his overhanging brows. "I know of you," he grunted. But he showed no fear, only caution.

It was increasingly apparent that this was no warrior of the decadent post-empire ilk. Var's technique was unconventional, but he was years younger than Neq, and much larger, so that even with his considerable stoop he stood taller. He had quick brute power, and the crude-seeming sticks were more solid than they looked, blocking sword-thrusts with considerable authority. The wood tended to catch the blade, holding it instead of bouncing it back, and that was dangerous indeed. The two sticks beat a tattoo on both his metal arms, their violent force bearing him back. Had his sword not been part of him, Neq could have been disarmed early, and certainly he was giving way before the onslaught.

Yet there was a certain eloquence about Var's attack, ferocious as it was. His balance was excellent. Without pausing, the man kicked off his boots and exposed horny bare feet—and then his footing was not clumsy at all. He was astonishingly agile for his bulk, yet his motions were economical.

A master sticker, in fact. Neq had encountered only two empire stickers with power and finesse like this. One was Tyl—greater on the finesse, less on the power—and the other was Sol . . . whose whereabouts Var must know.

But the sticks were not like the sword, and Neq's sword was not like others. His wrist was invulnerable. Though he was not young himself, he knew of no man who could match him in fair circle combat today, other

113

than Tyl. Var might hold him off for some time, but Var had to tire, to make mistakes, to overreach himself. The real strength of a sticker lay in his endurance under stress and his continuing judgment. There was where Neq had him: experience.

Neq fended off the blows and maneuvered for a clean opening himself. This was difficult, for Var danced about on his hooves and ducked his shaggy head sometimes almost to the ground—without ever exposing it.

"You are skilled, man of metal hands," Var muttered. "As befits a chief under the Master."

Neq eased his fencing, spying an opportunity to learn something. If Var were attempting to lull him by conversation, he would fail. "You are skilled too. I heard the Weaponless trained you himself."

"The Master is dead," Var said, relaxing his attack.

Neq let the pace slow, but remained vigilant. Var's companion might be near, ready to pounce treacherously during the double distraction of battle and dialogue. What kind of woman would mate with this kind of man, if not a beast-woman? "You could not have slain the Weaponless."

"Not in the circle," Var said grimly.

Neq stiffened. In that moment the sticker could have scored, had he been alert. Then the sparring resumed. "Sol of All Weapons followed you. You could not have slain him either."

"Not with the sticks."

This time Neq stiffened deliberately, proffering a seeming opening. Still Var did not strike. He was either too clever or too stupid. "You admit you killed them treacherously?"

"The radiation."

That blotched skin of his! Neq remembered now—there had been a story that the beast-boy could feel radiation, avoiding lethal concentrations himself while leading others into some badlands trap. So it was true, and Var had doomed both his friend and his enemy by luring

114

them through an unmarked radiation pocket! Now he dared to return with his bitch, thinking his crime unknown or forgotten.

So Neq's sources of information were gone. But there was one more thing to know. "Soli—the child of Helicon—"

Var actually smiled. "Soli exists no more."

Neq could hardly speak. "The radiation?" he whispered with biting irony.

But this question Var avoided, as though some lode of buried guilt had finally been tapped. "We have no quarrel. I will show you Vara."

Then the opening came, and Neq's sword struck true.

CHAPTER THIRTEEN

Tyl returned at dusk, with a companion. "Neq! Neq! Look what I found in the village!"

Neq looked up from the cairn he had been fashioning. As the two approached he saw that the stranger was a woman. "I'm so glad to find you!" she exclaimed.

Neq stared. It was a crazy woman! She wore the typical skirt and blouse despite the cold, and her long dark hair was bound the crazy way. And she was lovely.

"Miss Smith," he murmured, reminded achingly of his love though there was little actual, physical similarity between the two women. This one was neat to the point of precision, as Miss Smith had been; she was beautiful in that fragile manner; and she was incongruous in the wilderness. That was the connection. Intelligent, literate, innocent. His heart felt as though a dagger had nudged it.

"This is one of the two we traced," Tyl said. "She was reconnoitering in the village, the same as I, and when we met—"

"She traveled with a nomad?" Neq asked, still bemused by the parallel to his own experience of six years before. "A crazy?"

"I am Vara," she said. "I travel with my husband. He should be around here somewhere—"

Neq still had not come out of his fog. "Var? The Stick?"

"Yes! Did you meet him? From what Tyl says, we have a common mission—"

Then Neq came to total and ugly awareness. He touched the fresh burial mound with one foot. "I—met him."

Tyl looked at him and at the cairn, comprehending. His hand went to his sword, but dropped. He turned away.

Vara went to the cairn and carefully removed a section of the stone lining. She excavated the fresh earth and sand with her slender fingers while Neq watched. Finally she uncovered a foot, with its blunted, hooflike toes. She touched it, feeling its coldness.

By this time it was dark, and night closed in completely as she contemplated that deformed, dead foot. Then she covered it gently, filled in the hole, and replaced the stones.

"My two fathers are dead," she said wistfully. "Now my husband. What am I to do?"

"We met. We fought."

"I served Sol," Tyl said from his section of the night, still facing away. There was an anguished quality to his voice that Neq had not heard before. "I served the Weaponless. Var the Stick was my friend. I would have barred you from the circle with him, had I been certain of what I suspected. When I saw Vara, I was certain. But you met Var too soon."

"I did not know he was your friend," Neq said, hating this. "I knew him only as a slayer of men by treachery, and of a child at Helicon."

"You misjudged him," Tyl said in the same quiet tone

116

Vara had used. "He was bold in combat but gentle in person. And he had an invaluable talent."

"Var slew only of necessity," Vara said. "And not always *then*."

Neq was feeling worse, though it had been an honest combat. He had struck too hastily, as he had so often before. His sword outreached his intellect. He could have disengaged, waited for Tyl's return. Now he had to defend his action. "What need had he to slay the child of Sol?"

Vara turned to him in the dark. "I am the child of Sol."

Neq's stomach heaved with the pang of unwarranted killing, knowing what was coming. "He killed Soli at Mt. Muse, when she was eight years old. All accounts agree on that."

"All but one," she said. "The true one. He claimed to have killed me, so that the nomads would win, and my two fathers could be together again. But then I couldn't get back to tell Sol the truth, and the Weaponless was seeking Var for vengeance—"

"Vengeance!" Abominable concept!

"So we had to flee. We went to China, and I took his bracelet when I came of age. Soli exists no more."

Now Neq recognized her face, though it was no longer visible in the night. The classic beauty of Sola! The crazy dress and his own dawning guilt had blinded him to her identity.

"The boy Var traveled with, going north—" Neq murmured. "A girl with her hair hidden."

"Yes. So no one would know I wasn't dead. I can't do that now."

She certainly couldn't! The child of eight had become a woman of fifteen. "And Sol pursued you too, not knowing . . . he must have met the Weaponless on the way!"

"They learned in China. And gave their lives carrying radioactive stones into the enemy stronghold, so that we could escape. Var always felt that it was his fault they

117

died, but it was mine. I knew they would do it."

Var had blamed himself . . . and so had let Neq's accusation stand. Now Var's assumed guilt was Neq's.

"It was a mistake," Tyl said after a long pause. "Var told everyone he had killed the mountain champion. Helicon itself was fired and gutted to avenge that murder—it does not matter by whom. Neq did not know. Only *I* knew Var would not have slain a child. And I know the kind of terms Sola makes. She was kind to Var, but her price was surely the life of her daughter."

"Var did say something," Vara admitted. "He had sworn to kill the man who harmed me. And for a long time he was reticent, though he loved me. . . ."

Neq remembered Sola's comment about Var's sterility. Strange, driven woman!

"Yet I knew it could have happened," Tyl continued. "Mt. Muse is high and steep, and there are rocks to drop. Had you attacked him with stones while he was climbing, he might have had to fight before he knew, and he was deadly in rough terrain. So he *might* have killed you, and I could not bar Neq from combat until I was sure. It was my mistake; I am to blame for your husband's death—"

"No!" Neq and Vara cried together.

There was silence again, as each person sifted his tangled motives. The conversation was unreal, and not because it emanated from darkness. Neq's emotions were partly in suspension. "Why do you not curse me? Why do you not weep? I killed—"

"You killed because you did not understand," Vara said. "I have some share of guilt for that, for I agreed to play dead. Tonight I make you understand. Tomorrow I kill you. Then will I weep for you both."

She meant it. She was like Miss Smith, who died Neqa. Changed of name, precious beyond all imagination, but loyal to her man. Neqa had tried to kill Yod when Yod made ready to cut off Neq's hands. Would Vara do less?

Yod had killed Neqa by accident. Now Neq had killed

Var. The guilt was the same. Vengeance would be the same.

She would not have it, any more than he had. Neq bent his elbow, bringing his sword-arm to his own throat. It was past time for him to die.

"I claim my price," Tyl said, startling Neq as his muscles tensed for the fatal slice.

Of all times! Yet Neq had a debt of honor, and he would have to aquit it. "Name your price."

"Give back what you have taken this day."

Neq delayed answering, trying to discover Tyl's meaning. Obviously he could not restore Var to life.

"What you have to do," Vara said evenly, "do before dawn. When daylight comes I will destroy you in the circle."

"In the circle!" Now Neq could not fathom her meaning either. Women did not do battle. "What is your weapon?"

"The stick."

The morbid situation could not suppress Tyl's interest. "So Sol *did* train you in combat!"

"My father. Yes. Every day we practiced, inside the mountain. He hoped to take me away from Helicon some day, but Sosa wouldn't let him. And I have practiced since."

Now Tyl's voice was more concerned. "Mere practice can not make a woman into a man. My daughter is older than you, and she has a child of her own now—but this would never have come to pass if she had ever entered man's province. The circle is not for you."

"Nevertheless." Sol's child, all right!

"This man," Tyl continued persuasively, "this man, Neq the Sword, was second only to me in the empire, when the Weaponless departed. Now he has no hands, but he retains his weapon. He is less clever in technique, but more deadly than before because he cannot be disarmed. His sword is swifter than his mind. I think no man can stand against that sword today."

119

"Nevertheless."

"I can not permit this encounter," Tyl said.

Her voice was cold. "Your permission is irrelevant."

"Var was my friend. He taught me to use the gun. I hurt with his loss, as you do. Yet I say this: do not lift stick against Neq the Sword. We must not make this terrible mistake again."

"Var was more than friend to me," she pointed out caustically.

"Nevertheless."

"You have no right," she said.

Tyl did not answer, and the strange, tense conversation ended.

Neq did not know whether he slept that night, or whether the others did, but slowly the morning came.

Vara had changed. She no longer resembled an ineffective crazy woman. That guise must have been for the benefit of the local villagers, who were rather like crazies themselves in their dress, so that she could pass among them freely. Now she wore a nomad smock, and her hair was loose and long, falling down over her shoulders on either side and curling about the soft mounds of her breasts. She remained stunning by any definition.

She carried sticks—the twin thin clubs that Var had used.

Neq felt another chill. He had buried Var's weapon beside him, according to the normal courtesy of warriors. Neq's sword had cut open the ground and scooped it out, and his pincers had levered the stones into place: the work of several hours. Yet these were Var's sticks, for they carried the recent marks of the sword. Neq could recognize the scars of a weapon as readily as he could a face.

"As you fought my husband," Vara said, "so shall I fight you. As you slew him, so shall I slay you. As you buried him, I'll bury you. With honor. Then will my mourning begin."

"Neq will not fight a woman," Tyl said. "I know him, even as I knew Var."

Vara lifted her sticks and stood beside the burial mound. "He may fight or flee as he chooses. Here is the circle—beside my husband's cairn. The world is the circle. I will be avenged."

The words struck Neq like blows of the sticks. Her sentiments were so similar to his own when Neqa died! He could not have forgiven Yod and his rapist tribe; he had not forgiven them now. The thrust of his vengeance had changed, now applying to the entire outlaw society and its roots in the ashes of Helicon, but vengeance it remained. How could he say to her that a life for a life was not enough?

"Var was my friend," Tyl repeated. "He shamed me before my tribe when he was but a child, a wild boy of the badlands, and I meant to take him to the circle when he became a man. But Sola interceded on his behalf, and when I came to know him—"

Vara gripped her sticks and moved purposely toward Neq. He saw the savage grief in her eyes, the kind he had had, the kind that cast aside all thought of honor and permitted murder by stealth, the kind that was futile. But he had done it; he had killed without cause. He would not lift his sword to perpetrate further evil.

Tyl stepped between them. "Var was my friend," he said once more. "In any other case I would avenge him myself. Yet I forbid this conflict."

Vara did not speak. She whipped one stick at Tyl, a lightning stroke, her eyes not leaving Neq. It was no feeble womanish blow; lovely as she was, she did know the use of her weapon.

Tyl caught it on his forearm. "Now you have struck me," he murmured softly, though a massive welt was forming. Had there been a man's weight behind the blow, or had Tyl been unprepared for it, his arm could have been broken. "Now give me leave to fetch my weapon, for this conflict is mine."

Vara waited stonily. It was obvious she had not wanted to battle Tyl, and did not wish to engage him now. But she *had* struck him, and he had been unarmed —deliberately, for Tyl always knew where his weapons were. She was committed by the code of the circle.

Tyl fetched his sticks. Neq was relieved; had Tyl taken the sword to her, that death would have been charged to Neq's own conscience. Tyl intended only to interfere.

Yet why was he bothering? First he had balked Neq's own attempt at suicide; now he balked Vara. He was preserving Neq's life—when he should have been satisfied to see it end.

Now Vara threw off her smock and stood naked but for sturdy hiking moccasins, despite the chill of the air: as fine a figure of a woman as Neq had ever seen. She was full-breasted and narrow-waisted, well-muscled for a girl yet quite feminine. Her black hair flowed proudly behind her, almost to her hips.

Full bosomed . . . Neq was fascinated. Each breast stood round and true, a work of private beauty, an aspect of passionate symmetry. He had serenaded a breast like that, so long ago. . . .

It was fitting that such a breast now declared vengeance against him.

But Tyl stood between, and if Vara thought to dazzle him with her bodily attributes and so diminish his guard, she had forgotten that he had a daughter older than she.

She fenced with him, impatient at the delay Tyl represented. She wanted only to get at Neq, who had not moved.

The sticks spun and struck, wood meeting metal. Tyl had the advantage of superior Helicon weapons, and his experience was more than Vara's whole life. He parried her blows without effort.

Neq could not bring himself to care particularly about the fight or its outcome. The twin shocks of this final unjustified slaying of Var, and the identity and appearance of Vara, had almost completely unmanned him.

Discover what had gone wrong with Helicon? He could not discover what had gone wrong with himself!

Meanwhile, man and woman fought. Vara ducked and whirled about, her hair spinning about her breasts and hips like a light cloak. From that floating coiffure her sticks came up to rap sharply at Tyl's wrist, one side and another. A deft maneuver! Vara was, if anything, a better sticker than her husband had been.

But Tyl flicked his wrist out of the way and engaged in a counter maneuver that sent her stumbling back far less gracefully. "Very nice, little girl! Your father Sol disarmed me with a similar motion and made me part of his empire, before you existed. He taught you well!"

But there was more to the circle than good instruction, obviously. Tyl had never since been defeated by the sticks.

Had Neq been fighting, even with no guilt-related inhibitions, he would have been bemused by those dancing breasts playing peek-a-boo behind that black hair, and completely unable to strike at Vara's lovely lithe body. In fact he was bemused now. Her femininity was as potent in combat as her sticks.

Suddenly she turned away and kicked back, her heel striking for Tyl's knee. But again he moved aside in time. "The Weaponless—your other father?—crippled me with that blow when he was driving for the empire himself. But after my knees healed they became leary, and have not been injured since."

If Vara had not realized she was sparring with the top warrior of the old empire, she surely knew it now. Tyl was no longer young, but nothing short of Neq's sword had hope of moving him out of the circle. Vara was fifteen and female; those were insurmountable obstacles.

Tyl was merely blocking, of course. He had no interest in hurting this beautiful girl; he only meant to convince her that she could not have her way.

Vara required considerable convincing. She whirled, she feinted, she sent a barrage of blows against the man.

She knew an astonishing variety of tricks—but there was no trick that could overmatch Tyl's reach and strength and experience.

Finally, panting, she yielded far enough to speak. "Warrior, what is it you want?"

"Neq slew Var in fair combat. Even as I could disarm you now, so could Neq defeat Var. I would not face Neq with the stick myself. Forswear your vengeance."

"No!" she cried, and launched another flurry of blows at him.

"No!" Neq also cried. "It was not fair combat. Var withheld his attack, he opened his guard, saying we had no quarrel. Then I slew him."

Tyl retreated, dismayed by the words rather than by the girl's offense. "This is not like you, Neq."

"It is too much like me! I have slain innocent men before. I did not understand in time. I thought it was a combat mistake, or a ruse. My sword was there—"

"Desist, girl," Tyl said, just as though she were his daughter playing a game. And Vara desisted. "Neq, you place me awkwardly."

"Let her have her vengeance. It is fair."

"That I cannot."

"You admit you slew him unguarded!" Vara blazed at Neq.

"Yes. As I have others."

"In the name of vengeance!" Tyl cried, as if proving a point.

"In the name of vengeance." Neq was sick of it.

"In the name of vengeance," Vara repeated, and now the tears showed on her cheeks.

"Yet you could have slain him fairly," Tyl said. "And you thought you were avenging—her."

"I misunderstood. I did not let him explain. I slew him without reason, and I am tired of slaying, and of the sword, and of life." Neq faced Vara. "Come, widow. Strike. I will not lift weapon against you."

"If you strike him thus," Tyl said to her, "you become

guilty of the same crime you avenge. Knowingly."

"Nevertheless," she said.

"Understand him first—only then are you justified. Learn what he is, what he contemplates."

"What can he be, what can he plan, that will repay what he has stolen from me!" she cried.

"Nevertheless."

She cried, she cursed in Chinese, she threw her sticks at the ground; but she was already committed. As was Neq.

CHAPTER FOURTEEN

"Melt that?" the smithy cried incredulously. "That's Ancient-technology steel! My forge won't touch it!"

"Then sever it," Neq said.

"You don't understand. It would take a diamond drill to dent that metal. I just don't have the equipment."

No doubt an exaggeration, for Helicon had made the weapon. But these northerners were closer to the past wonders than were the nomads, having houses and heaters and even a few operating machines, and so they stood in greater awe of the Ancients. Neq himself stood in awe, after learning what had been done at Helicon. Perhaps this smithy was superstitious; at any rate, he would not do the job.

"I must be rid of it," Neq said. As long as his sword remained, he was a killer. Who would fall next—Vara? Tyl? Dr. Jones? The sword had to go.

The smithy shook his head. "You'd have to cut off your arm at the elbow. And that would probably kill you, because we don't have medical facilities in this town for such an operation. Find the man who put that sword on you; let him get it off again."

"He is three thousand miles away."

"Then you'll just have to wear it a while longer."

Neq looked at his sword-arm, frustrated. The shining blade had become an anathema to him, for while he wore it he was inseparable from his guilt.

He looked about the shop, unwilling to give up so readily. Metal hung from all the walls—horse shoes, plowshares (so *that* was what the crazies had suggested he make his sword into, facetiously!) axes, bags of nails. All the products of the smithy's art. The man was evidently competent; he must make a good living, in the fashion of these people who worked for recompense. In one corner dangled a curved piece of metal with a row of little panels mounted along a center strand. Neq could envision no possible use for it.

The smithy followed his gaze. "Don't you nomads believe in music?"

"A harp!" Neq exclaimed. "You made a harp!"

"Not I," the man said, laughing. He took it down fondly. "This is no harp; it has no strings. But it *is* a musical instrument. A glockenspiel. See—these are chimes—fourteen plates of graduated size, each a different note. I traded a hundred pounds of topgrade building spikes for this. I'm no musician, but I know fine metalwork! I've no idea who made it, or when—before the Blast, maybe. You play it with a hammer. Listen."

The smithy had become quite animate as he described his treasure. He fetched a little wooden hammer and struck lightly on the plates. The sound was like bells, seldom heard in the crazy demesnes. Every tone was clear yet lingering, and quite lovely.

Neq was entranced. This evoked old and pleasant memories. There had been a time when he was known for his voice as well as his sword . . . before the fall of the empire and horrors thereafter. He had sung to Neqa. . . .

He could not make his sword into a plowshare, obviously, but it gave him an idea. He did not have to cut off his weapon; he merely had to nullify it. To make it impossible for him to fight.

"The glock and spiel—fasten it to this sword so it won't come off," he said.

"To the sword! A marvelous instrument like this?" The smithy's horror was genuine.

"I have things to barter. What do you require for it?"

"I would not sell this glockenspiel for barter or for money! Not when it is only going to be destroyed by a barbarian with no appreciation for culture. Don't you understand? *This is a musical instrument!*"

"I know music. Let me have your little hammer."

"I won't let you close to an antique like this! Get out of my shop!"

Neq started to raise his sword, but caught himself. This was the very reaction he sought to quell: sword before reason. He had to *convince* the smithy, not intimidate him.

He looked about again. There was a barrel of water near the great anvil, and he was thirsty. He had walked all day with Tyl and Vara, and come into this village on sudden inspiration when he saw the smithy shop. If the man could only be made to understand. . . .

> All day I faced the barren waste
>   without the taste of water—
> Cool, clear, water!
> Dan and I with throats burned dry
>   and souls that cry for water—
> Cool, clear, water!

The smithy stared at him, astonished. "You can sing! I never heard a finer voice!"

Neq had not known he was going to sing. The need had arisen, the mood fit—and a silence of six years had been broken. "I know music," he said.

The man hesitated. Then he pushed the glockenspiel forward. "Try it with this."

Neq took the manner awkwardly in his pincers and tapped a note. The sound thrilled him, more perfect than any voice could be. He shifted key to match, striking the same note steadily to make a beat.

> The nights are cool and I'm a fool
> each star's a pool of water—
> Cool, clear, water!

The smithy considered. "I would not have believed it! You want this to play?"

Neq nodded.

"Price was not my objection. I see you would have trouble playing the glockenspiel in the wilderness, unless it were attached. Yes. It *could* be done . . . I would have to coat the blade with an adhesive . . . but you would never be able to fight again. Do you realize that?"

They bargained, and it was done. He became Neq the Glockenspiel.

"A *what*?" Vara demanded, surprised and suspicious. "You have beaten your sword into a *what*?"

"A glockenspiel. A percussion instrument. My sword was too bloody."

She faced away angrily. Tyl smiled.

They traveled south and east. Tyl and Neq were returning to make their report to Dr. Jones. Vara, though she did not see it that way, *was* that report. She was the only one remaining who could answer the necessary questions about the nature of Helicon's demise. But she thought she was coming to have her vengeance on Neq; she did not mean to let him escape.

Tyl did not start any conversations. Neq hardly felt like talking himself, and Vara remained sullen. They had about three thousand miles to go: between three and four months at their swift pace. It was not likely to be a pleasant trip.

But they had to work together, for the natives were generally unfriendly and the old hostels no longer existed even in the formal crazy demesnes. They were cutting across what had been known as western Canada, intending to skirt the southern boundaries of a series of large lakes, and the northern boundaries of the worst badlands. Tyl had a crazy map; it claimed such a route existed.

Someone had to forage each day for food; someone had to stand guard each night; someone had to get them safely through outlaw territories. Tyl did most of it at first. Then Vara, shamed, began to help.

Neq, stripped of his sword, could neither fight nor forage effectively. He was dependent on the other two, and mortified by the situation. It was hard to give up a weapon, and not merely in the circle! All he could do was keep watch—and for that he had to stay awake. That was not easy after a twelve hour hike, each day.

One night as they camped by a river, Neq consoled himself by striking the tip of his pincers against the bells of his glockenspiel. He had not tried to play it since leaving the smithy's shop. But the sound was not proper; metal on metal annoyed him. He took the little wooden hammer and tapped the notes experimentally, regaining the feel of the music. Soon he was running through the scales, improving his competence while the others slept. It was possible to play entire melodies with no more than the hammer! He began to hum, measuring his voice against the clear tones of the instrument. It was there in him yet: the joy of music.

Finally he unstopped the voice that had been dormant during the entire time of killing, and that had emerged only when his sword was buried. He sang, accompanying himself carefully on the glockenspiel:

> Then only say that you'll be mine
> And our love will happy be
> Down beside some water flow
> By the banks of the O-hi-o.

He sang all of it, though this was not that river and his voice, despite the smithy's compliment, was imperfect now, a creaky shadow of its prime. But the instrument gave him a certainty of key he had not had before, and the spirit of the melody suffused him with its odd rapture.

As he sang, he rocked to the lovely, tortured vision of it: the young woman taking a walk by the river strand, refusing to marry the suiter, being threatened by his knife at her breast, and finally drowned. An ugly story, but a beautiful song—one of his favorites, before he had come too close to living it. There were tears in his eyes, making his watch difficult.

"Your wife—did you kill her too?"

He was not startled to find Vara awake. He had known he could not sing aloud without arousing her curiosity or ire. "I must have."

"I ask only because I have to," she said bitterly. "Tyl balked me, on pain I should know you. Before I kill you. I saw you had no bracelet."

"She was a crazy," he said, not caring what she might think about Neqa.

"A crazy! What have you to do with them?"

"I thought to rebuild Helicon."

"You lie!" she cried, clutching at her sticks, which were always with her, warrior-style.

Neq looked at her tiredly. "I *kill*. I do not *lie*."

She turned away. "I may not kill you yet."

"You want the mountain dead?"

"No!"

"Then tell me: what is Helicon to you? Were you not kept prisoner there, and betrayed at the end? Don't you hate it yet?"

"Helicon was my home! I loved it!"

He studied her in the moonlight, perplexed. "Do you want it restored, then, as I do?"

"No! Yes!" she cried, crying.

Neq let it be. He knew what grief was, and the burning for revenge. And futility. Vara was in the throes of it all, as he had been when Neqa died. As he was still. It

130

might be months, years before she made sense to others or to herself, and she would not be so pretty, then.

He tapped the flat metal bells of the glockenspiel again, picking out a new tune. Then he sang, and Vara did not protest.

"I know my love by her way of walking
   And I know my love by her way of talking . . ."

Tyl slept on, though their conversation was not quiet.

"When I first saw Var," Vara said, "he was standing on the plateau of Mt. Muse, looking down from the rim. He could have dropped a rock on me, but he didn't, because he wasn't the kind to take advantage."

"Why should anyone drop a rock on you?" Neq demanded, disliking this reference to the dead man.

"We were meeting in single combat. You know that."

"Why did Bob send a child?" Was the truth at last within reach?

"And after we fought, it was cold, and he held me so I would not shiver. He gave me his heat, for he was always generous."

They were working at cross purposes.

"Would you warm your enemy if he were cold?" she asked him.

"No."

"You see. Var was a giver of life, not of death."

She had meant to hurt him, and she had succeeded. How could he return to this bitter girl what he had taken from her?

"Ambush," Tyl murmured. "Well-laid; I saw it too late. You two break while I cover the retreat."

Neither Neq nor Vara reacted openly; both were too well versed in tactics. They exchanged a glance of chagrin, for neither had been aware of the situation. But if Tyl said there was an ambush, there was an ambush, though the forest seemed deserted.

131

Vara turned nonchalantly and started back. Neq shrugged and followed, while Tyl whistled idly and moved toward a tree as though for a call of nature. But it was too late; the trap sprung, and they were neatly in it.

From front, back and sides armed men appeared and converged. They carried clubs and staffs and sticks. No blades, oddly. Now Neq understood how the three had walked into the trap: the ambushers came out of holes in the ground! The trapdoors were flush with the forest floor and covered with leaves so that nothing showed until they opened.

But this was a great deal of trouble for a mere ambush! And no sharp weapons! Why?

Tyl and Vara had run together the moment the men appeared. Now they stood back to back, sticks in each hand. Neq remained where he was; his first abortive motion to uncover his sword had reminded him that he was no longer armed. If he joined the other two he would only hamper them.

The men closed in. Neq remembered the similar maneuver of a tribe six years before, closing in on a truck. If he could have known in time to save Neqa . . . !

"Yield," the leader of the ambush said.

No one answered. They were too wise in the ways of outlawism to doubt that death would be cleanest in battle. Such elaborate preparations would not have been made merely to recruit tribesmen!

"Yield or die!" the leader said. A ring formed about the two stickers, and another around Neq. "Who are you?"

"Tyl of Two Weapons."

"Vara—the Stick."

The ambusher considered. "Only one Tyl of Two Weapons I know of, and this is pretty far out of his territory."

Tyl didn't bother to answer. His sticks remained ready; his sword hung at his side.

"If it *is* him, we won't take him alive," the leader said. "*Or* his woman."

Vara didn't deign to correct him. Her sticks were ready too.

"Why would he travel without his tribe?" another man inquired. "And with a girl young enough to be his daughter?"

"*That's* why, maybe," the leader said. He came over to Neq. "But this one doesn't talk, and he covers his weapon. Who are you?"

Slowly Neq raised his left arm. The loose sleeve fell away and the metal pincers came into view.

There was a murmur in the group. The leader stepped back. "I have heard of a man who had his hands cut off. So he had his sword grafted on, and—"

Neq nodded. "They were ambushers."

The circle about him widened as the men edged away.

"We have a gun," the leader said. "We do not want to kill you, but if you move—"

"We only pass through," Neq said. "We have no business with you." He was now talking to distract attention from Tyl, who might then get out his own gun unobserved. There were enough men here to overcome the little party, though that would not have been the case had Neq's blade been in place and Tyl's gun ready. The outlaw's gun was not the advantage they supposed.

"You *have* business with us," the leader said. "We require a service from you. Perform it and you shall go free with the wealth of our tribe on your shoulders. Fail it, and you shall die."

Neq ached with fury to be addressed in this manner, as though any threat by any straggling outlaw could move him. He had destroyed a tribe of such arrogance before. But he had given up the sword. Now he would live or die without it. "What is your service?"

"Walk the haunted forest at night."

Neq stifled a laugh. "You fear ghosts?"

"With reason. By day the forest harms no one, and

stands athwart our richest hunting-grounds, just a few miles down this trail. But the ghosts strike those who enter at night. First the blades, then the dull weapons. Banish our spook: walk it at night and live. We will reward you richly for breaking the spell. Our food, our equipment, our women—"

"Keep your trifles! Feed us today; tonight we challenge your ghost. Together. Not for your sake, but because it crosses our route."

"You will keep your sword covered in our camp?"

"I keep my arm covered if no man annoys me."

"And you?" the leader called to Tyl.

"And I," Tyl agreed, and Vara also nodded.

Slowly the encircling men lowered their weapons.

As the sun descended they were ushered to the edge of the haunted forest. It seemed normal—mixed birch, beech and ash, some pine, with pockets of pasture heavily grown. Rabbits scooted away from the party. Good hunting, certainly!

"Are there radiation markers near here?" Tyl inquired.

"Some. But that danger is over. We have a click-box; the kill-rays are gone."

"Yet men still die," Tyl murmured.

"Only by night."

That certainly didn't sound like radiation. It didn't come and go; it faded slowly, and was not affected by daylight.

"If Var were here—" Vara began. And caught herself.

"It is about ten miles," the tribe leader said. "We have a smaller digging downstream. Sometimes we need to travel between the two at night—but we must hike twice as far, over the mountain. No one passes the valley by night."

"The river looks clean," Tyl observed. "Your footpath is open?"

"Throughout. There are no natural pitfalls, no killer-animals here. Once there were shrews, but we exterminated them. Now there are deer, rabbits, game-birds. No hunting animals."

"You have found bodies?"

"Always. Some without marking. Some mutilated. Some dead fighting. We never send a man alone or unarmed, yet all perish."

So they ambushed innocent travelers to send here, Neq thought. Very neat, but none too clever. Hadn't it occurred to them that whoever conquered the haunted forest might have second thoughts about the manner he had been introduced to it? He might decide on a bit of vengeance. In that case, solution of the forest riddle could be disastrous for the tribe.

Tyl began to walk. Neq and Vara followed quickly. It was not dark yet, but night would set in long before they got through the forest. A ten mile hike by night, rested and fed—routine, except for ghosts!

When they were well away from the tribesmen, they split, ducking down out of sight on either side of the trail. No word was spoken; all three were conversant with such technique. The greatest danger might be from the men behind, not the supposed ghosts in front. Strangers might be deliberately killed in the forest to sustain the notoriety of the region, for surely the tribesmen could not be entirely ignorant of the nature of the threat, whatever it was.

But no one was following. Cautiously the three proceeded, Tyl flanking the forest side of the trail, Vara following the river side, and Neq, who could not fight, moving cautiously down the center. He held a thin stick in his pincers, probing for deadfalls, and he walked hunched to avoid a potential trip-wire or hanging noose. He expected to encounter something deadly, and not a ghost!

In an hour they had covered less than two miles. Their extreme caution seemed to have been wasted; no threat of any kind materialized. But eight miles remained, and eight hours of darkness. The fear of the tribesmen had been genuine; perhaps they delved underground because of a lingering terror of the forest surface.

The way was beautiful, even at night. The somber trees overhung the path to the west, highlighted by the full moon, and the river coursed slowly on the east side, and great vines covered with night-blooming flowers lay along the ground. The heavy fragrance surrounded them increasingly, musky and refreshing in the slight breeze.

Neq recalled his childhood. It had been nice, then, with his family and his sister. All the subsequent glory and ruin of empire could not compare with that early security. Why had he left it?

Hig the Stick! The man had cast his lustful gaze on Nemi, Neq's young twin sister! Neq clenched his sword-hand in reminiscent fury and bravado—and remembered he had no hand. Yod the Outlaw had taken it—

Time twisted about. It was dark, but Neq could see well enough in the diffused moonlight. A shape was coming at him, and it was the shape of Yod. Yod, whose foul loin had—

Neq whipped up his gleaming sword and launched himself at the enemy. A head would ride the stake to-night!

Contact! But his sword did not handle properly. It clanged, a discordant jangle.

Shocked, he remembered. No sword! This was the glockenspiel, for making music.

He peered more carefully at his opponent. "Tyl! Do you raise your sword to me in anger?"

Startled, Tyl stepped back. "Neq! I mistook you for—someone else. But he is dead. I must be overtired. I do not raise my sword to you."

Mutually shaken, they retreated from each other. How could such a confusion have come about? Had the glockenspiel not sounded, they might easily have fought, and Tyl could have slain him unwittingly. What irony, when they had not yet even encountered the menace of the forest!

reminding himself that what he saw was false. He began to pick out a tune, there in the water—the water that seemed like rich warm blood—and the notes were lovely and clear. They expanded to form a melody, each note bearing its private animation but the theme expanding to encompass the world. The tune was marching; each beat was a bright foot. He saw them treading into the sky.

He sang:

> "You must walk this lonesome valley
> You have to walk it by yourself!
> Oh, nobody else can walk it for you . . ."

The melody took hold of him compellingly, carried him up out of the river, gave him a glorious and sad strength.

> "We must walk this lonesome valley—"

Shapes came at him, male and female . . . but the music daunted them. Like a cordon of warriors, the band of notes swept back the opposition, softened its determination. He sang and sang, more wonderfully than ever before.

> "We have to walk it by ourselves
> Oh, nobody else can walk it for us . . ."

Then, hesitatingly, the shapes joined in.

> "We have to walk it by ourselves . . ."

With burgeoning confidence Neq started another sequence, marching down along the path while his body dripped wet water and the others followed.

> "Takes a worried man
> To sing a worried song!"

and the ghost-echo agreed, and they sang together, louder.

> "It takes a worried man
> To sing a worried song!
> I'm worried now,
> But I won't be worried long!"

Victoriously, Neq continued, throwing new forces of song and music into the fray as the old troops lost their potency against the ghost-fragrance. On down the path, through the dark forest, singlemindedly dispelling the insidious fumes with voice and instrument, leading the captive shapes out of the lonesome valley.

Then it was done. Embarrassed, Neq broke off his singing, finding his voice hoarse. They had walked and sang for hours. Tyl and Vara were there, shaking their heads as though waking from nightmare.

Dawn was coming.

CHAPTER FIFTEEN

"Stay clear of the tribesmen," Tyl said. "Let them think we are dead, or they may kill us to preserve their secret. We'll sleep in the forest today."

"The haunted forest?" Vara demanded nervously.

"It is safe by day. We shall want to visit it again by night."

Again!" Neq was incredulous. "We nearly killed each other there! The ghosts—"

"You spared us that," Tyl said. "Your weapon vanquished them and brought us out. But our conquest is not complete until we know what causes the effect, and why the outlaw tribe chooses to sacrifice ignorant strangers to it. Surely they know; they can not be so stupid as to spend their lives adjacent to it and not fathom the mystery. I have never fled from an enemy—or left a potential enemy behind me."

He was right. An enemy neglected was doubly dangerous. "The flowers," Neq said. "Night bloomers."

Tyl removed his weapons. "Sticks to you," he said to Vara. "Sword to you, Neq."

Neq could not hold the sword effectively in his claw, but he understood what Tyl was doing.

Tyl went to a hanging vine and plucked a closed bud. He pulled it open and put it to his nose. He sniffed. "Faint—not the same." He sniffed again, deeply. Then a third time.

His manner changed. His eyes widened, then narrowed. His hand went for his sword.

Then he grinned and dropped the flower. "This is it!" he cried. "I'm high on it now—but I know what it is. Don't come near me—"

They knew what he meant. The weak, temporary daylight effect of one bud might not overcome a forewarned man, any more than an ounce of alcohol would. But the massed fragrance of thousands of blooms, in the flush of their strength, building up all night long—that would be another matter.

"I don't think we'd better stay the night," Vara said. "It fuels our passions. . . ."

Yes. And there was already a matter of death-vengeance between them.

Tyl went down to the river and dunked his head. He came back dripping but triumphant. "We know the haunt now!"

"We still have to breathe at night," Neq said, returning the sword. "We got through once, but it would be foolhardy to risk it again."

Tyl considered. "Yes. I knew what it was doing to me, just now, but I didn't care. If I had had my weapons—"

"It was the same with me last night," Neq admitted. "But all I had was song."

"The *flower* is the weapon," Tyl said. "One that would

141

bring down a tribe. If others knew of it, it would be planted everywhere. We must make it ours."

Vara rubbed her eyes. None of them had slept yet, and the tribesmen could soon appear. Tyl was probably correct: the tribe had more interest in maintaining the secret of the forest than in exposing it. Dead men would spread its reputation, and prevent other tribes from moving in on the good hunting preserve. Naturally only strangers would be sacrificed. It was time to hide and sleep.

Tyl nodded. "We'll make a baffle by the water, under the bank, and sleep together without posting guard. If they find us, we'll stall until dusk—or dive into the river."

The tribesmen were either too confident or too stupid to search thoroughly. No one found them. Refreshed, the three walked to the southern fringe as the blooms opened. No tribesmen stood guard, understandably.

"If light makes them close . . ." Tyl murmured.

Neq jumped. Tyl was leading the way directly to a large group of the opening flowers! "Careful—moonlight didn't stop them last night."

"Maybe it *did*," Vara said. "Maybe that's why we got through. We got only part of the effect. . . ."

"Stand upwind," Tyl said. He brought out his light. It was a small kerosene lantern with a circular wick and adjustable mantle, and it had a spark-striker attachment. It had been cumbersome to carry, and Tyl had seldom used it before, preferring his own night vision. He had never been one to travel unprepared, however.

He ignited the lantern, adjusted it for maximum brilliance, and brought it near the vine. There was a reflector, so that a surprising amount of illumination was concentrated in that vicinity.

Slowly the flowers closed.

"If light seals them, darkness must open them," Tyl said. "If we carried a vine with us—"

"It would die," Neq said, leary of the notion.

"A growing vine, with its earth. Set in a box with this light."

"A weapon!" Vara exclaimed, catching on. "Cover it by day, leave it among enemies. . . ."

Tyl nodded. "Pick it up when they are dead. Turn on the light. Travel on."

"A counter-ambush," Vara finished, her eyes seeming to glow in the night.

More killing, Neq thought. No end to it, whether with sword or flower. Yet the plan had merit. "This is a fringe zone. Will it grow beyond this forest?"

"Delicate mutation," Vara said excitedly. "Needs the right temperature, water, soil, shade—"

"We'll find out," Tyl said. "Man has tamed plants before."

The two of them hastened to dig up an appropriate sample and fix its enclosure. Neq had qualms, however. Any oversight, and the flowers could wipe out their little party. This was an uncertain ally.

"Var was self-sacrificing," Vara said. "He always helped me, even when I was pretending to be a boy. When we slept in the snows and I was stung by a badlands worm, he carried me back to the only hostel though his own ankle had been turned. And he fought to preserve my rest, though he was not then fit for the circle. He was exhausted and his foot was swollen—"

Neq had to listen. This was the man he had killed. He could not restore what he had taken without first comprehending her loss. He understood what she was doing: Tyl had stopped her from attacking him with the sticks, so now she turned to words. Her voiced memories were terrible because they brought a dead man back to life, multiplying Var's greatness and the agony of his demise.

Her verbal campaign was calculated, and he knew it, but still it hurt him. He had no legitimate defense. He had killed her husband, the man who should have been his friend, and now could never be.

Sometimes when she said Var he heard Neqa. Neq himself had become Yod: slayer of the innocent.

* * *

143

It worked. The vine prospered under Tyl's care, and a minimum flame in the lantern kept the narcotic flowers closed. But normally they set the plant down some distance from their night camp and let it bloom, so that its natural cycle would not be unduly disrupted. They had no concern about animals bothering it; the fragrance was defense enough. A mile's separation seemed more than sufficient—less than a mile when the wind was sure—though upon occasion they smelled the faint perfume and felt a token enhancement of animal passion.

They did encounter another ambush, as such things were too common in this post-crazy world. They managed to barricade themselves defensively for an hour, using Tyl's gun to keep the outlaws at bay, while the covered vine slowly opened its flowers and poured its essence forth through vents in the box. Neq sang and played his glockenspiel when he felt the effect, confining himself to songs of solidarity and justice while the fragrance wafted into the afternoon air. Tyl and Vara joined him, laying their weapons on the ground under their feet, out of sight of the enemy. The ambushers laughed, thinking the whole show ludicrous.

Then the enemy warriors fell to quarreling among themselves. The fumes had spread. They were not strong, but the ambushers were aggressive and unsuspecting. Tyl uncovered the vine to let in daylight, for they had to be free of the effect themselves before moving out. They were on guard against their own raw emotions, but there was no sense taking chances.

The ambushers were in disarray, not comprehending the reason. The strong passions of men driven to outlawry had been sufficient. Once the conflict started, it fed on itself.

Neq made the mistake of singing a love song. He became acutely conscious of Vara next to him, almost sixteen and at the height of her womanhood. He became sexually excited, not caring what else had passed between them. But Tyl was there, and in the sudden fierce

144

resentment of the man's interfering presence Neq realized the danger and forced himself to shift songs. Love Vara? Safer to kiss a badlands kill-moth!

It was time to move out. "Onward Christian Soldiers!" Neq sang. The words were incomprehensible, but the tune and spirit were apt.

They marched singing through a wilderness of carnage. Only occasionally did they have to defend themselves from attack. Some pairs were locked in combat, some in amour, for the women had been drawn into the activity. A man and a woman snarled and bit at each other in the midst of copulation. Children were fighting as viciously as adults, and some were already dead.

The passion would pass, but the tribe would never quite recover.

Vara's campaign continued. Neq learned how Var had saved her from a monster machine in a tunnel—the same tunnel Neq had lacked the courage to enter—and from a hive of wasp-women, and how he had interposed his body to take arrows intended for her. He had fought the god-animal Minos to save her from a fate almost as bad as death.

Var had evidently had a short but full life. The documentation of that life was sufficient to cover more than a month of travel, at any rate. The climate became warmer as they moved south and east and further into spring, but the girl's language never ameliorated.

When she finally ran out of Var's virtues, she started on Var's faults.

"My husband was not pretty," Vara said. "He was hairy, and his back was hunched, and his hands and feet were deformed, and his skin was mottled." Neq knew that, for he had fought the man. "His voice was so hoarse it was hard to understand him." Yes. With clearer enunciation, Neq might have understood enough in time to withhold his thrust. "He could not sing at all. I love him yet."

Gradually Neq got the thrust of this new attack. Neq himself was handsome, apart from the lattice of scars he had from years of combat and the mutilation of his hands. His voice was smooth and controlled. He could sing well. Vara held his very assets against him, making him ashamed of them.

It was like the vine narcotic. Neq knew what she was doing, but was powerless to oppose it. He had to listen, had to respond, had to hate himself as she hated him. He was a killer, worse than the man who had killed his own mate.

Tyl did not interfere.

In the next month of their travel, Vara grew especially sullen. Her campaign was not working, for Neq only accepted her taunts. "I had everything!" she exclaimed in frustration. "Now I have nothing. Not even vengeance."

She was learning.

She was silent for a week. Then: "Not even his child."

For Var had been sterile. Her father Sol had been castrate; she had been conceived on his bracelet by Sos the Rope, who later gave his own bracelet to Sosa at Helicon. So her husband, like her father, had had no child.

Neq knew that twisted story, now, and understood why the Weaponless, who had been Sos, had pursued Var. Vengeance, again! But Var had been hard to catch, for his discolored skin had been sensitive to radiation, a marvelous advantage near the badlands. But that ability had come at the cost of fertility.

"And my mother Sosa was barren," Vara cried. "Am I to be barren too?"

Tyl looked meaningfully at Neq.

Var had been naive. Neq was not. That had been established and reestablished in the past two months, to his inevitable discredit. But this shocked him. The meaning of Tyl's original stricture had suddenly come clear.

Vara wanted a baby. . . .

She didn't seem to realize what she had said, or to

comprehend why Tyl had stopped her from attacking Neq at the outset.

Yet what was in Tyl's mind? If he thought it important that Vara have her baby, there were other ways. As many ways as there were men in the world. Why this? Why Neq, Vara's enemy? Why dishonor?

There was an answer. Vara did not want just a baby—she wanted a child to Var. Any infant she bore would be Vari, the line of Var. Just as she herself had been born Soli, child of the castrate Sol. The bracelet, not the man, determined parentage in the eyes of the nomads. And what man would abuse Var's bracelet and his own honor by contributing to such adultery, however attractive the girl might be?

What man indeed—except one already shed of his bracelet, and so hopelessly sullied by his own crimes that violation of another bracelet could hardly make a difference? What man, except one bound by oath to return a life taken?

What man but Neq!

CHAPTER SIXTEEN

Now it was Tyl's turn to advance his cause, and Neq's to stand aside. The trek continued into the third month, interrupted by strategies and combats and natural hazards, but the important interaction was between Tyl and Vara. Vara's initial fury had been spent, and she was now vulnerable.

It started subtly. One day Tyl would ask her a question, seemingly innocuous, but whose answer forced her to consider her own motivations. Another day he would question Neq, bringing out some minor aspect of his background. In this way Tyl established that Vara's closest ties were to Sol, not her biological father, and to Sosa, not her natural mother, and that Sol and Sosa had lived together in deliberate violation of both their bracelets, making a family for Soli/Vara.

"It's different in Helicon," she said defensively. "There are no real marriages there. There aren't enough women. All the men share all the women, no matter who wears the bracelets. It wouldn't be fair, otherwise." She spoke as though Helicon still existed, though she knew the truth.

"Did Sosa share with all the men, then?" Tyl inquired as though merely clarifying a point of confusion. "Even those she disliked?"

"No, there was no point. She couldn't conceive. Oh, I suppose she took a turn once in a while, if someone insisted—she's quite attractive, you know. But it didn't mean anything. Sex is just sex, in Helicon. What counts is that women have babies."

Similarly true in the nomad society, Neq thought.

"Suppose you had stayed there?" Tyl asked.

"Why should I be different? I was only eight when I left, but already—" She stopped.

Tyl didn't speak, but after a while she felt compelled to explain. "One of the men—there's no age limit, you know. He liked them young, I suppose, and there weren't many girls anyway. But I wasn't ready. So I hit him with the sticks. That was all. I never told Sol—there would have been trouble."

There certainly would have been! Neq remembered something she had cried in the flower-forest, when the visions were strong. A threat to some attacking man.

"But if you had been older—" Tyl said.

"I would have gone with him, I guess. That's the way it is, in Helicon. Preference has nothing to do with it."

"But when you married Var—would you have returned to the mountain then?"

"That was where we were going!" Then she had to

explain again. "Var would have understood. I would have kept his bracelet."

But she shared some of Var's naivete, for she still didn't comprehend where Tyl was leading her.

Neq's turn as subject, then, in similar fashion. Day by day, as they marched and fought and slept. He didn't want to cooperate, but Tyl was too clever for him, phrasing questions he had to answer openly or by default. Gradually the outline of Neq's service in the empire came out, and his extreme proficiency with the sword, and the code by which he had lived. Yes, he had killed many times as a subtribe leader, but never outside the circle and never without reason. Much of it had been done at Sol's direction; none on order of the Weaponless, who had not tried to expand the empire.

Vara remained grim, not liking this seeming alignment of character.

Then Tyl came at Neq's post-empire activity. "Why did you seek the crazies?"

"The empire was falling apart, and so was the nomad society, and outlaws were ravaging the hostels. There was no food, no supplies, no good weapons. I tried to learn why the crazies had retreated."

"Why *had* they retreated?"

"They depended on supplies from Helicon, and their trucks weren't getting through. So I said I'd take a look."

Then the description of what he had found at the mountain. Vara's impassivity crumbled; tears streamed down her cheeks. "I knew it was gone," she cried. "My two fathers did it, and Var and I helped. But we didn't know it was that awful. . . ."

Thus Tyl had somehow cast Neq as the upholder of civilized values, while Sol and the Weaponless and even Var were its destroyers. What a turnabout for Vara's assumptions!

They marched a few more days. Then Tyl resumed. "Did you go alone to Helicon?"

Neq would not answer, for the memories remained raw

149

despite the years and he did not want this part of it discussed.

Surprisingly, it was Vara who pursued the questioning now. "You married a crazy! I remember, you admitted it. Did she go with you?"

Still Neq was silent. But Tyl answered. "Yes."

"Who was she? Why did she go?" Vara demanded.

"She was called Miss Smith," Tyl said. "She was secretary to Doctor Jones, the crazy chief. She went to show the way, and to write a report. They drove in a crazy truck, all the way across America. That's the Ancient name for the crazy demesnes—America."

"I know," she said shortly. And another day: "Was she fair?"

"She was," Tyl said. "Fair as only the civilized are fair."

"*I'm* fair!"

"Perhaps you too are civilized."

She winced at the implications. "Literate?"

"Of course." Few nomads could read, but most crazies had the ability. Vara herself was literate, but neither Tyl nor Neq.

Another day: "Was she a—a real woman?"

"She turned down the Weaponless, because he wouldn't stay with the crazies."

Neq winced this time. Neqa had put it another way.

"The Weaponless was my father!" Vara flared. Then: "My natural one. Not my real one."

"Nevertheless."

"And she loved Neq?" she demanded distastefully.

"What do you think?" Tyl asked in return, with a hint of impatience.

Another day: "How could a literate, civilized woman love *him*?"

"She must have known something we do not," Tyl said with gentle irony.

Finally: "How did she die?"

Neq left them then, afraid to discover how much Tyl knew. The man was embarrassingly well versed in Neq's private life, though he had given no hint of this before.

Neq ran through the forest until he was gasping for breath, then threw himself down in the dry leaves and sobbed. This merciless reopening of the old, deep wound; this sheer indignity of public analysis!

He lay there some time, and perhaps he slept. As darkness came he saw again the bloody forest floor, felt again the fire of severed hands. Six years had become as six hours, in the agony of Neqa's loss.

What use was it to practice vengeance, when every tribe was as savage as the one he had destroyed. Any one of those outlaw tribes could have done the same. The only answer was to ignore the problem—or to abolish them all. Or at least to abolish their savagery. To strike at the root. To rebuild Helicon.

Yet here he was, after having tried his best to organize that reconstruction, subject to the bitterness of a girl who saw him as the same kind of savage. With reason. How could a savage eliminate savagery?

It was all useless. None of it could recover the woman he had loved. The body lay there, tormenting him, mocking his efforts to reform. The musky perfume of the vine-lotus enhanced its horror. He didn't care.

After a time he rose to bury the corpse. *He* was a savage, but Dr. Jones was civilized. Neq could not help himself, but he could help the crazies. He had loved one of them—this one. To that extent he loved them all. He bent to touch the body, knowing his hand would strike something else, whatever it was that was really there. A stone, perhaps.

The flesh was there, and it was warm. It was a woman. "Neqa!" he cried, wild hope surging.

Then he knew. "Vara," he muttered, turning away in disgust. What preposterous deceit!

She scrambled up and came after him, circling her arms about his waist. "Tyl told me—told me why you killed. I would have killed too! I blamed you falsely!"

"No," he said, prying ineffectively at her arms with the

151

heel of his pincers. "What I did was useless, only making more grief. And I did kill Var." The fumes were stronger. She looked like Neqa.

"Yes!" she screamed, clinging as he moved. "I hate you for that! But now I understand! I understand how it happened."

"Then kill me now." As so many had begged *him*, when he stalked Yod's tribe. "You have honored Tyl's stricture."

"But *you* haven't!" Her grip on him tightened.

"The vine is here. I smell it. Let me go before—before I forget."

"I brought the vine! So there would be truth between us!"

He batted at her arms with the closed pincers. "There can be no truth between us! Tyl would have us defile our bracelets—"

"I know! I know! I know!" she cried. "Be done with it, Minos! Set me free!" She climbed him, reaching for his face with her mouth. She was naked; she had been that way when he first touched her, as she played corpse.

The flower drug sang complex melodies within his brain, making him overreact on an animal level to this female provocation. He crushed her to him within the living portion of his embrace, joining his lips to hers.

It was savagely sweet.

She relaxed, fitting more neatly within the circle of his arms. The glockenspiel jangled against the pincers, jolting him into momentary awareness of their situation. In that moment he wrenched away from her. His body was aflame with lust, but his mind screamed dishonor! He ran.

She ran too, fleetly. "I hate you!" she panted. "I hate your handsome face! I hate your wonderful voice! I hate your fertile penis! But I have to do it!"

In the dark he smashed into brush and spun about, trying to avoid the tangle. She dived for him again. He fended her off with the claw, trying not to hurt her but determined to keep her at bay until the narcotic wore off.

As long as she was desirable to him, he had to balk her ardor.

Now *she* was fighting *him*. She had fetched a stick along the way, a branch of a tree, and she struck him about the shoulders with it, hard enough to hurt. He knocked it away, then caught it in the pincers and wrenched it loose by superior strength. But her hands remained busy, striking him on nerves so that the pain was excruciating. She had the combat art of the Weaponless, all right!

Yet muscle and experience counted heavily, and they both knew that Neq could subdue her at any time merely by striking her hard enough with his claw. She was not really trying to defeat him; her intent was to maintain physical contact until her sexuality became irresistible.

But they had left the vine behind. The air was clear, here, and so was his head. Neq saw no more visions, and reacted nomally. He had won.

Realizing this, Vara stopped abruptly. "So it didn't work," she said, as though she had merely stubbed her toe. "But I tried, didn't I?"

"Yes." How was it possible to comprehend her thought processes!

"So now it's real."

"Yes." He started to get up.

She was crying, with real tears. "You monster! You denied me my love, you denied me my vengeance, you even denied me my rationale. Are you going to deny me my humiliation too?"

Hers no more than his! "Yes."

She flung herself on him again, kissing him with her teary face, bearing him back against the brush. There was blood on her body where the branches and thorns had scraped her. "I call you by your name! Neq. Neq the Sword! No artifice between us. No deceit."

"No humiliation!" he said.

"No humiliation! Do you take me now as a woman—or do I take you as a man? *It shall be!*"

It had been a long time, she was highly desirable, and

153

there were limits. Neq sighed. He, too, had tried. "It shall be."

They made love quickly, she doing more than he because he could not use his hands.

"I never completed the act with her," he said, both satisfied and bitter. "She was afraid...."

"I know," Vara said. "As were you." Then: "Now we have done it. Now there is no onus. Stay if you wish."

"It is only sex. I do not want to love you."

"You have loved me for a month," she said. "As I have you. Stay."

Neq stayed. It was the first time he had completed the act with *any* woman, and she must have known that too, but she did not show it. Gradually they explored each other, letting down the physical and emotional barriers. They did not talk; it was no longer necessary.

The second time it was much better. Vara showed him some of what she knew, and she seemed to be as experienced in this respect as he was in battle. But mostly it was love, unfettered.

CHAPTER SEVENTEEN

The trip was done. The three reported to Dr. Jones at the crazy building. Tyl, the tacit leader, did the talking, summarizing Neq's search for missing people, Tyl's own trek with Neq, their encounter with Var and Vara, and their journey back—except for the dialogue and romance.

"Neq has renounced his sword," Tyl concluded. "He wears the glockenspiel now. Yet he retains the capacity for leadership."

Dr. Jones nodded as though something significant had been said. "The others will no doubt take the matter under advisement."

Tyl and the crazy leader went to round up the "others." Neq and Vara took the vine outside where there was more light. They settled under a spreading tree.

"Tyl will be master of Helicon," Vara said. "See how close he is to the crazies."

Neq agreed. "He brings people together."

"You and I came together inevitably," she said with feminine certainty. "Helicon was your idea. You should be master."

"With this?" He uncovered the glockenspiel.

"You could change it back. The sword is still there, underneath."

It was too complicated to explain that he never had been considered for the Helicon office. "If I wore the sword again, you would have to kill me."

She frowned, surprised. "I suppose I would."

A little boy about four years old wandered by, spotting them. "Who are you?" he asked boldly.

"Neq the Glockenspiel."

"Vara the Stick."

"I'm Jimi. You have funny hands."

"They are metal hands," Neq said, surprised that the boy had not been frightened. "To make music."

"My daddy Jim has metal guns. They make bangs."

"Music is better."

"It is not!"

"Listen." And Neq lifted the glockenspiel, took the little hammer in his pincers, and began to play. Then he sang:

> A farmer one day was a traveling to town
> Hey! Boom-fa-le-la,
>   sing fa-le-la,
>   boom fa-le-la lay!
> Saw a crow in a fir tree way up in the crown
> Hey! Boom fa-le-la,
>   sing fa-le-la,
>   boom fa-le-la lay!

"What's a town?" the boy inquired, impressed.

"A nomad camp with crazy buildings."

"I know what a boom falela is! A gun."

Vara laughed. "I want one like him," she murmured.

"Find Jim the Gun, then."

"After this one," she said, patting her abdomen.

Neq, startled, sang another verse for the boy.

> Then the gun from his shoulder
>   he quickly brought down . . .
> And he shot that black crow
>   and it fell to the ground . . .

"I told you guns were better!"

> The feathers were made
>   into featherbeds neat . . .
> And pitchforks were made
>   from the legs and the feet . . .

"How big was that crow?" Jimi inquired, fascinated.

Neq struck a loud note. "About that size."

"Oh," the boy said, satisfied. "What's that thing?"

"A flower vine."

"It is not!"

"The flowers only open in the dark. Then they smell funny, and people do funny things."

"Like crows with pitchforks?"

Vara laughed again. "Just about," she said.

Tyl emerged from the building. "They're ready."

Vara picked up the vine-pot and they went inside. Jimi followed. "He has funny hands," he informed Tyl. "But he's fun."

They were all there: the group of odd-named oldsters he had rounded up, along with Dick the Surgeon, and Sola, and several more he did not know. Apparently Dr. Jones had located more of the people on the list during Neq's absence. Some were nomads, male and female.

Jimi went to one of these, evidently Jim the Gun.

Vara, poised until this moment, took Neq's covered arm. "Who's that?" she whispered, nodding specifically.

"Sola," he replied before realizing the significance of her identity. The woman had recovered more than a suggestion of her former splendor.

Vara clutched his arm as though terrified. It was entirely uncharacteristic of her.

Tyl stepped in and performed the introduction. "Sola ... Vara. You have known each other."

Sola did not make the connection, for she had not known of Var's marriage. But the others saw the resemblance as the two women stood together. "Mother and daughter ..." Dick said.

"Widows, both," Tyl said. The words seemed cruel, but they were not, for this clarified a prime source of concern and confusion at once. No further questions about that matter would be asked. That meant in turn that the more devious and less honorable relationships would not be exposed.

Yet it was awkward. Sola and Vara had parted perhaps thirteen years ago, when Vara was hardly more than a baby. What was there to say?

Once more Tyl interceded. "You both knew Var well. And Sol. And the Weaponless. As I did. Soon we must talk together of great men."

"Yes," Sola said, and Vara agreed.

"In your absence," Dr. Jones said to Neq, "we located a few more volunteers, as you see. We have screened them as well as we could, and believe they represent a viable unit. Provided suitable leadership develops."

"There are leaders here," Neq said. Did the crazy want him to affirm his support for the leader already chosen?

"The destruction of the prior Helicon suggests that its leadership was inadequate," Dr. Jones said. "We have been obliged to make certain restrictions."

Neq pondered that. Apparently he was being asked not only to support, but to nominate the leader! "You won't work with just anybody. But you can work with Tyl—"

"I return shortly to my tribe," Tyl said. "My job is done. I am not of this group. I would not leave the nomad culture or take my family under the mountain."

Neq was amazed. So Tyl, too, had been merely supporting the effort, not directing it!

"I know of Jim the Gun," Neq said. "He armed the empire for the assault on—"

"I made a mistake!" Jim broke in. "I shall not make another. I know better than to command what I once destroyed."

Apparently Dr. Jones had not set things up so neatly after all! "What are your requirements?" Neq asked the crazy. "Literacy? Helicon experience? What?"

"We would have preferred such things," Dr. Jones admitted. "We would have liked very much to have found the Weaponless. But other qualities are more important now, and we must work with what we have."

"Why not Neq?" Vara asked.

Neq laughed uncomfortably. "My leadership has become a song. I shall not kill again."

"That is one of our requirements," Dr. Jones said. "There has been too much shedding of blood."

"Then you require the impossible," Neq said grimly. "Helicon was built on blood."

"But it shall not be *rebuilt* on blood!" Dr. Jones exclaimed with unseemly vehemence for one of his character. "History has clarified the folly of violence and deceit."

Many of the people in the room were nodding agreement. But Neq thought of the way the outlaws would have to be tamed, and knew the dream of nonviolent civilization was untenable.

"Neq the Sword," Sola said after a pause. "We know your history. We do not condemn you. You say you shall not kill again. How can we believe you, when your whole way of life has been based on vengeance by the sword?"

Neq shrugged. He saw already that no man who could

give the absolute assurance of pacifism they demanded could be an effective leader of Helicon. He could not kill by his own arm, but he had agreed to the indirect slaughter of the flower vine during the trek here. His stance against killing had been hypocritical.

"Take him as your leader!" Vara exclaimed. "All of you are here because of him!"

"Yes," one thin old crazy agreed. "This man lifted an outlaw siege against my post, and took a message for me that brought rescue. I trust him, whatever else he has done."

Jim the Gun spoke. He was a little old nomad with curly yellow hair. "We do not question Neq's capacity. We question his judgment under pressure. I myself was ready to shoot somebody when I learned how my brother had died in Helicon—but I did not. A man who would go berserk for weeks at a time, whatever the provocation—"

"I like him," Jimi said. "He has music hands."

Startled, Jim looked at his son. "That man is Neq the Sword!"

"He says music is better'n guns. But I like him."

"We share your vision," Sola said to Neq. "But we must have a leader of inflexible temperament. A man like the Weaponless."

"The Weaponless destroyed Helicon!" Vara flared. "Can anybody even count how many men died because of him? Yet you say no killing, and you want—"

Sola looked at her sadly. "He was your father."

"*That's* why he did it! He thought I was dead. You talk about a few weeks berserk—He planned it for *years*, then he followed Var for years. *Nothing had happened to me!* And you—you sent Var to kill the man who might harm me, when no one *had*. Who are you to judge? But Neq saw his wife—Dr. Jones' own secretary, a beautiful and literate woman—Neq saw her raped by fifty men, and then they cut off his hands and dumped him in the forest with her corpse. He should have died then—but he brought that tribe to justice. Now he wants to stop *all*

159

outlaws by rebuilding Helicon. And you hypocrites quibble about the past!"

"Where is Var the Stick?" Sola asked quietly.

Vara couldn't answer.

"I slew him," Neq said.

Their faces told the story. Many of these people had known Var, and more had heard of him. They were hardly ready to accept his killer as their leader. And why should they?

"It was an accident," Tyl said. "Neq thought Var had killed Soli in her childhood, as we all thought. He reacted as we all did. Before he learned the truth, Var was dead. Because of that error, Neq put aside the sword. Now I speak for his sincerity—and so does Vara."

"So we noticed," Jim said, in a tone that made Vara flush furiously.

Jimi was looking at the vine.

"Show your weapon," Tyl said to Neq.

Neq unveiled the glockenspiel. There was a murmur of amazement, for none of them had seen it before.

"Use it," Tyl said.

Neq looked about. The faces were grim and sad—grim for him, sad for Vara, who was crying without shame. These people evidently shared his vision of a new Helicon, but the example of the prior one frightened them. It frightened him too, for he had seen it in ruins.

Perhaps Helicon could not function without bloodshed, direct or indirect. Perhaps there was no way to restore the old society. But it had to be tried, and now was the time, and this was the group. He could not let it all slide away just because of the confused scruples of the moment.

They needed a leader. If he did not assume command, no one would. He was far from ideal, but there was no one else.

Neq turned to Dr. Jones. "You asked me to find out why Helicon perished, so that we could prevent it from happening again. How did the leadership fail? I do not know. Perhaps it will fail again. Perhaps Helicon is doomed. But this is a risk that must be taken."

Dr. Jones did not respond.

Neq looked for his little hammer, but couldn't find it. So he tapped out a melody slowly with the pincers, touching the glockenspiel lightly so as to avoid the unpleasant metallic effect. Then he sang.

> If I had a hammer,
>   I'd hammer in the morning.
> I'd hammer in the evening
>   all over this land.
> I'd hammer out danger,
>   I'd hammer out warning!

As he sang, he looked first at one person, then another. The song had special meaning for him, as every song did, and while the melody was venting itself through his lung and mouth and instrument he believed it. Its pre-Blast originators could not have honored its precepts—but he was hammering out warning.

It was as though he were meeting each man in the circle and conquering him with his syncopation. And each woman was vulnerable to the sincerity of the song, the vibrant emotion of it. While his voice and hammer were in harness Neq the Glockenspiel was potent even in the face of their unified distrust.

> I'd hammer out love
>   between all my brothers
>   all over this land!

He finished that song, and sang another, and then another. It was as though he were marching out of the haunted forest again, and in a way he was, for there was nothing but song to do the job that had to be done. Vara began harmonizing with him, the way Neqa had done long ago, and slowly the others formed into a circle about him, compelled to echo the words.

He sang. The very room wavered and flowed, shaping itself into an ugly badlands mountainside girt by tangled metal palisades, irregular stone battlements, a tunnel under the awful mountain, a vast cavern filled with ashes. Helicon formed, and Helicon's promise infused the group. From death came life—the mountain of death that meant life for the finest elements in man. The dream became tangible, thrilling, eternal; a force that no living man could deny.

At last he stopped. They were his, now, he knew. His dream had met their caution and prevailed, however illogically. Helicon would live again.

Then he saw the vine-box. Jimi had covered it, so that the flowers had opened in their darkness, and the narcotic had seeped into the room while Neq was singing.

Tyl must have seen it happen, and let it be, for Tyl was gone.

CHAPTER EIGHTEEN

Fifty strong, they unloaded at devastated Helicon. The mountain appeared much the same from the outside—a looming, forbidding mound of refuse.

"We shall not need to kill in Helicon's defense," Neq said. "We will accept those who climb to the snow line. If they are unsuitable, we will send them far away. No one who comes to us must be allowed to return to the nomad world."

The others nodded. They all knew the mischief such returns had made in the past. Had Helicon truly kept to itself, instead of dabbling in nomad politics, the original society of the crazy demesnes would have survived unbroken. It had been a lesson—one that Neq himself had learned most harshly of all.

The nomads were the real future of mankind. The crazies were only caretakers, preserving what they could of the civilization the nomads would one day draw upon. Helicon was the supplier for the crazies. But Helicon and the crazies could not make the civilization themselves, for that would be identical to the system of the past.

The past that had made the Blast. The most colossal failure in man's history.

Yet by the same token the nomads had to be prevented from assuming command of Helicon, either to destroy it or to absorb its technology directly. There must not be a forced choice between barbarism and the Blast. The caretaker order had to be maintained for centuries, perhaps millennia, until the nomads, in their own time, outgrew it. Then the new order would truly prevail, shed of the liabilities of the old.

That, at least, was Dr. Jones' theory. Neq only knew that they had a job to do. Perhaps the others understood it better than he did, for even the scattered children in the group were subdued.

"To many of you, the interior will be strange," Neq said. "Think of it as a larger crazy building, gutted at the moment but about to be restored by our effort. Each person will have his area of responsibility. Dick the Surgeon will be in charge of group health, as he was before; he will check the perimeters with the radiation counter— the crazy click-box—and set the limits of safety by posting warners. Only with his permission—and mine—will anyone go beyond these. The mountain is a badlands; the kill-spirits still lurk.

"Jim the Gun will be in charge of mechanical operations: restoring electric power, making the machinery functional. Most of us will work under his direction for as long as it takes. A year, perhaps. Without the machinery Helicon can not live; it will bring in air and water and keep the temperature even and make our night and day. Some of you are—*were*—crazies; you know more about electricity than Jim does. He's in charge because he's a

163

leader and you are not. Had there been leadership among the crazies, Helicon might never have fallen, and would certainly have been rebuilt before this."

They nodded somberly. Leaders existed among the nomads, but the crazies didn't operate the same way. In time the new Helicon would amalgamate its disparate elements and rear its own leaders and technicians and be a complete society in itself. Right now everything had to be makeshift.

Neq continued announcing assignments while the others stared at the mountain. Cooking, explorations, foraging, supply, cleanup—he had worked this out carefully in consultation with literate crazy advisers during the truck journey here, and he wanted each person to know his place in the scheme as he viewed the interior for the first time. He put Vara in charge of defense, for the time being: she would cultivate the vines, and clear rooms for the flowers to occupy, and set up an effective system of lights and vents so that no one could penetrate Helicon by stealth without passing through that narcotic atmosphere. The mountain would never be taken by storm! Sola was in charge of boarding; she had to assign a private room to each man, and provide for some recreational facilities.

"What about rooms for the women?" someone asked.

"We have no rooms," Sola said. "We will share with the men—a different room each night on strict rotation. That is the way it has to be, since we have only eight women within the nubile range, and forty men. There is no marriage here, and bracelets are only sentiment. You all knew that before you enlisted."

Then Vara described the history of Helicon, for the majority of this group was aware of only portions of it. She told how the Ancients, who had been like crazies with nomad passions, had filled the world with people they could not feed and had built machines whose action they could not control, and had finally blown themselves up in desperation. That was the Blast—the holocaust that had created the contemporary landscape.

Not all the people had died at once. More were killed by radiation than in the physical blast—actually a massive series of blasts—and that had taken time. There were desperation efforts to salvage civilization, most of which came to nothing. But one group in America assembled an army of construction equipment and bulldozed a mountain from the refuse of one of the former cities. It was the largest structure ever made by man, and probably the ugliest—but within its depths, shielded from further fallout, was the complex of Helicon: an enclave of preserved civilization and technology. Only a tiny portion of this labyrinth was residential. A larger section consisted of workshops and hydroponics, and one wing contained the atomic pile that generated virtually unlimited power.

"Dr. Jones assures us that's still functional," Vara said. "It's completely automatic, designed to operate for centuries. It made the first century, anyway. All we have to do is reconnect the wiring at our end."

The name Helicon had been borrowed from a myth of the Ancients: it was the mountain home of the muses, who were the nine daughters of the gods Zeus and Mnemosyne, and were themselves the goddesses of memory and art and science. Poetry, history, tragedy, song—it all reflected the spirit of Helicon as originally conceived. The virtues of civilization were to have been remembered here.

But Helicon had lacked self-sufficience in one vital respect: personnel. The people who first stocked it had been the elite of the devastated world: the scientists, the highly skilled technicians, the ranking professionals. Most were men, and most were not young. The few women, children of the elite, could hardly replenish the enclave in a generation without dangerous inbreeding—and they had substantial scruples about trying.

So it was necessary to allow limited immigration from the outside world. The prospect was appalling to the founders, for it meant admitting the very barbarians that Helicon was on guard against, but they had no choice. Without enough children to educate in the traditions and technology of civilization, Helicon would slowly die.

They were fortunate, for some elements of civilization had survived outside. People who later came to be known as the "crazies" because their idealistic mode of operation made no sense to the majority, were quick to appreciate the potential benefits of collaboration. They provided some new blood for Helicon, and pointed out that many barbarians could be safely recruited if they were made to understand that there was absolutely no return. Thus Helicon became the mountain of death—an honorable demise for those with courage. And regular, secret trade was instituted, with Helicon adapting a portion of its enormous technical resources to the manufacture of tools and machinery, while the crazies provided wood and surface produce that was much preferable to the hydroponic food turned out by less-than-expert chemists.

The crazies' vision turned out to be larger than that of the founders of Helicon, for the crazies were in touch with the real world and were necessarily pragmatic about nomad relations, despite the nomads' opinion. They ordered weapons from the Helicon machine shops—not modern ones, but simple nomad implements. Swords and daggers; clubs and quarterstaffs. They issued these to the nomads in return for a certain docility: the weapons were to be used only in formal combat, with noncombatants inviolate, and no person could be denied personal freedom.

Enforcement was indirect but effective: the crazies cut off the supply to any regions that failed to conform. Since the metal weapons were vastly superior to the homemade ones, the "crazy demesnes" spread rapidly as far as their supply lines were able to go. Their services expanded to include medicine and boarding, with hostels being assembled from prefabricated sections produced in Helicon. There was nothing the crazies could return in direct payment for Helicon's full-scale help—but the improvement in the local level of civilization was such that many more recruits were available for both the crazies and Helicon. All three parties to this enterprise profited.

But Helicon remained the key. Only there could high-quality items be mass-produced.

Then Helicon had been destroyed. And the crazy demesnes had collapsed.

"And ours was the best system in the world," Vara concluded. "There are other Helicons in other parts of the world, but they were never as good as ours and they don't have much effect. Var and I discovered that in the years we traveled. To the north they have guns and electricity, but they are not nice people. In Asia they have trucks and ships and buildings, but they—well, for us, our way is best. So now we are going to rebuild Helicon . . ."

Neq took them inside by way of the passage from the hostel. "This will be our secret," he said. "Converts will have to try the mountain. But the crazies can't send trucks up there, so they will bring supplies for trade to this point. This hostel is seldom used by nomads in the normal course, since it is an end station, not a travel station."

The tunnel curved into its darkness. The lift is on hostel power," Neq explained, reminded again of Neqa and her explanations to him so long ago. "Once we restore Helicon power . . . but lanterns will do for now."

When they were gathered in the storage room, he opened the panel to reveal the subway tracks. A wheeled cart was there; he had brought it up when he finished the long grisly cleanup job. Only a few of the party could ride it at a time, and it had to be pushed by hand, but it was still quicker to ferry them this way than to make them all walk. The nomad converts in particular were nervous about these depths.

When all were assembled on the platform at the other end, he guided them up the ramp for the grand tour. The nomads were awed, the crazies impressed, and the Helicon survivors subdued. Everything was bare and clean—no doubt quite a contrast to what the former underworlders remembered.

At the dining hall he paused, feeling a chill himself. He remembered the way he had left it, after removing the bodies and cleaning out the charred furniture. He had stacked the salvageable items in one corner, and had left a cache of durable staples in the kitchen area.

One of the tables had been moved. Some of his dried beans had been used. Someone had been here.

Neq concealed his dismay by continuing the tour. "I don't know the purpose of all the rooms, and certainly not the equipment," he said. "We'll be drawing heavily on the experience of those of you who were here before."

Inwardly he was chagrined. He and the crazies had searched for every possible surviving member of Helicon. Compared experiences and his body-count suggested that very few were unaccounted for. Was the intruder from outside? Most of the tribesmen were terrified of this region, and would never enter the mountain even if they could find their way in.

Of course Tyl and his army had forced entry here during the conquest of the mountain, so those men could penetrate Helicon again if they chose. But Neq had sealed over the invasion apertures as well as he could and none of them seemed to have been reopened, and no damage had been done.

Someone had come without fear, looked about, had a bite to eat, and departed. That person could come again.

CHAPTER NINETEEN

"Yes, she is pregnant," Dick the Surgeon said. "I think under the circumstances she should be excused from, er, circulation. Our children will be our most important asset for some time, for they will be raised in the atmosphere of civilization. . . ."

It was Neq's decision to make, and it would set a precedent, but he was aware of his own bias. Intellectually he knew that the women had to be shared; emotionally he couldn't share Vara. "It's a matter of health," he said. "That's your department."

So Vara did not circulate. Actually the system had not been fully implemented yet; people needed time to settle in to it. There was some problem about the women's arrangements, for they required more privacy than the men's rooms provided, sexual aspects aside. Finally they were assigned rooms of their own, but were expected to make their rounds on schedule.

If the social system functioned with hesitation, at least the reconstruction didn't. The restoration of electric power was much simpler than anticipated. A few cables replaced, a few circuit-breakers closed, a few fixtures tinkered with, a few parts substituted, and there was light and heat and circulating air and sanitary facilities in operation. Helicon had been beautifully designed; they were not building or even rebuilding it. They were merely implementing a system that had been temporarily interrupted. In a month they were ready to tackle the peripheral machinery: the subway to the hostel, the manufacturing machines. In two months the first weapons were produced: quarterstaffs cut from an endless metal pole extruded from an automatic smelter-processor. There was ore from the monstrous metallic refuse of the mountain—enough for a century's such operations.

Neq realized with a certain surprise that it was working! Helicon was coming back to life, beginning to function again. That simple, significant success had almost been obscured behind the minutiae of daily projects and crises! Actually, Helicon was an entity in itself, performing in its own fashion; the hiatus of years and the change of personnel seemed almost irrelevant to its giant personality.

The signal alarm woke Neq during the night cycle. Night was artificial here, as was day, but they maintained the same rhythm as above. The recently renovated television screen was on.

"We've netted something," Jim the Gun said tersely. "It didn't pass through any of the entrances we know, but it's inside now. I thought you'd want to be on hand."

"Yes!" Neq shrugged into his special open-sleeve robe and hurried through the half-lighted halls to Jim's laboratory. He remembered the mysterious visitor. Had he come again?

"I thought it was one of the fringe beasts," Jim said. "They keep finding new places. . . ." Neq knew what he meant. There were strange creatures in the radiation-soaked outer tunnels of the mountain—mutation-spawned monsters who had shaped their own grotesque ecology. Helicon proper had been sealed off from such sections, but the seal was imperfect, and sometimes rodents and amphibians got through. Once a dead toothy froglike thing had popped out of a flush toilet, and Jim had had to trace the sewer pipes to discover the entry point. It had been hopeless; Helicon's water came from a vast subterranean conduit and departed the same way after passing through a waste-recycling plant. It was too complex to unravel, and dangerous to tamper with, for the water was hot—so hot that live steam burst periodically from vents and filled the maintenance passages. Jim had had to settle for a filter in the main drinking-water pipe. Sometimes eerie noises penetrated the walls, as of alien creatures hunting or struggling. The increasing hum of functioning machinery drowned much of this out, and that was a blessing. It was too easy for the nomads to believe in haunts—since, of course, there *were* haunts.

Jim had rigged an alarm system designed to spot the emergence of any such creatures, so that the holes could be located and plugged. "It's a big one this time," he said, leading Neq to a storeroom as yet unused. The back wall here seemed solid, but Jim had traced skuff-marks in the dust of the floor to a removable panel constructed to resemble stone. "Human or near-human, obviously," Jim said. "He came in from the other side—it seems to be a half-collapsed tunnel with some radiation—and pushed out the panel, then replaced it perfectly. Then on through the room and out to the hall—which is where he tripped my electric-eye system. He was gone by the time I got here, of course—but at least we know how he did it."

Neq felt the chill again. "But he's inside Helicon—right now!" Had he come for beans again—or something more?

Jim nodded. "He passed the eye half an hour ago. I can't tell from the signal whether it's a mouse or an elephant—uh, that's an extremely large animal that existed before the Blast. Elephant. I get several of these each night—"

"Elephants?"

"Alarms. And I don't know anything until I check personally. Half the time it's one of our own personnel, on some unscheduled business. Or a couple of them. Quite a bit of out-of-turn trysting in these back rooms, you know. I have to be very cautious about checking. The girls share, but they want to get pregnant by particular men . . ."

Neq knew. He had never cracked down on it because

171

he felt the same way himself. It was *his* baby Vara carried, whatever name it was to bear.

"So we're late starting, but we can run him down. Block off this exit and flood the halls with flower-narcotic—"

Neq didn't like it. "There are *people* going about," he pointed out. "We keep a limited night shift going now, and some are on the machines. A whiff of the flower, and equipment could be wrecked. The amount that gets around by accident is bad enough! No, we'll do it by hand. How could a stranger come, and not be seen?"

"He would have to know Helicon," Jim said. "Where to hide, where to step aside—"

"And how to bluff his way through when he *did* meet people," Neq said. "That makes him dangerous. We don't know his motive."

"It has to be a former member of Helicon," Jim said. "One of our retreads should be able to recognize him?"

"Helicon is open to the old members. Why hasn't he contacted us?"

"Maybe he's trying to."

"All he has to do is yell or bang on the wall."

"Let's go to my lab," Jim said. "If he keeps ducking out of sight, he'll have to trip other alarms."

They were in luck. The intruder tripped several alarms, ducking out of the way as others used the hall. Jim kept no eye-beams set in the main passages, since that would lead to hopeless confusion. It was coincidental, but his emplacements were ideally suited to this type of chase.

"He's going somewhere," Jim said. "See that pattern. I think he's literate—a couple of those dodges were near the dining room bulletin board. Now he knows what he wants. When we figure it out too, we'll be able to intercept him. Catch him by surprise, so he can't hurt anyone."

"Toward the sleeping quarters!" Neq exclaimed, looking at the chart of Helicon on which Jim had set his markers.

"Oh-oh. I don't have them bugged, for the obvious reason. We'll lose him."

"I'll post emergency guards." And Neq went about the matter quietly, using the underground intercom system to wake those on call. Soon armed men would stand at strategic points in all the halls of that section.

But *soon* was not *now*. A horrible picture formed in Neq's mind. The person who would have known Helicon best was its former leader, Bob. He would have escaped if anyone had. Neq used his office now, and was reminded of the man more than he liked. There were little things about the setup, such as the way the metal desk faced the only door, and the gun in that desk, and the wiring for intercom connections to every part of Helicon, and the spotlights set in the ceiling. That office was a little fortress. There had been scorch-marks in it, as in the rest of Helicon—but no corpse. Sol could have caught Bob elsewhere and killed him, of course—but there was no proof of that. Bob might have survived, somehow—and now he could be returning, determined to be avenged on the child who had rejected his perverted advances. . . .

Abruptly something else came clear. *That was why Bob had sent Soli to her presumed death!* Vengeance for the embarrassment she had caused him! Instead of submitting, she had driven him off with her sticks . . . and at any time she could have told Sol. She had had to be eliminated—and what better way than by besieging nomads, Sol's kind?

And therein lay Bob's fatal mistake. He had not acted for the best interests of Helicon, but to avenge and cover his own mistake with Soli. He had let personal factors interfere with his duty.

"What?" Vara exclaimed as Neq entered. "Oh, it's you."

Just as Neq was letting his own involvement with the same girl interfere with his own duty. "There's a stranger in the halls, coming this way. For you, I think. There wasn't time to set guards—"

173

"Oh!" she said, going for her sticks.

He pushed her down on the bed again. She was heavy and her breasts were huge as he touched her in the dark. "No action for you! That's why I'm here. If he enters—"

"But I have no enemies, do I?" she asked. "Except maybe you, when I empty my belly and start sharing in a few months."

He laughed, but the remark cut him. How could he enforce the system for others, unless he honored it himself? No wonder the social system had not been working well.

Bob's mistake. . . .

"It is over between us," he said. "I love you, but I am master of Helicon. I must be objective. Do you understand?"

"Yes, you are right," she said, and it hurt him that she could agree so readily. "It has to be that way."

He knew then that it *was* over. She was a child of Helicon; she understood the sharing system emotionally as well as intellectually. She had never been his to keep.

A few minutes later they both heard it. Quick furtive steps in the hall, coming near.

The door opened. Neq raised his claw to strike, wishing for his sword. He nudged the light switch with his elbow. Brilliance erupted.

Vara screamed.

Momentarily blinded, the stranger stood with tousled hair and arms lifted on guard. A woman. Naked.

Pretty face, rather shapely figure, lithe legs, well formed breasts—had he had his sword, he would have cut her down before he realized.

"Sosa!" Vara cried, scrambling from the bed.

The two women embraced while Neq stood with claw frozen. Of all the developments!

"Oh, mother, I'm so glad!" Vara sobbed. "I *knew* you were alive . . ."

Sosa: the woman Vara considered her real mother, in preference to Sola. Naturally she had returned to join her

174

daughter. Naturally she didn't care about anyone else. Or to meet anyone else, in her silent nudity. She just wanted to visit Vara and perhaps take her away, staying clear of other entanglements. She had probably had to swim through some of the fringe-cavern waterways, avoiding radiation. The mystery had been solved.

Now the two women were reunited, and oblivious to him. Neq left quietly, knowing he would not be missed.

Vara did not leave. Sosa stayed. She merged with the group so smoothly that it seemed she had always been there. She assumed Vara's duties including the sharing, and though she was of Neq's generation the men were very glad to participate with her. She was a small, active woman in very good condition and easy to get along with. Her immediate past was a mystery; she had disappeared when Helicon was destroyed, and reappeared now that it lived again, and she confessed her troubles to no one.

If Neq had doubted Vara's need for him before, now there was no question. Vara needed nobody but Sosa. It was good that such comfort was available in her period of stress, but it cast Neq loose without even the excuse of jealousy.

Jim's call on the newly-renovated television network awakened Neq again. Another routine emergency!

"Someone in the subway," Jim said. "Going, not coming. Seems to be female."

Vara, he thought, horrified. Sosa had finally talked her into leaving, so that the baby would not be subject to Helicon! "I'll check it myself," he said.

Jim nodded in the screen, perhaps understanding Neq's concern. It was a matter to handle privately.

Someone was certainly in the subway, but not using the cars. Neq let out the breath he had held when passing through the flower-chambers and smelled the other faint perfume, the kind the women liked to wear. Of course she would not use one of the cars; such a drain on

Helicon power would immediately alert the monitor. Few people knew about Jim's *other* monitors, as a matter of policy and security. Increasingly Neq appreciated the various mechanisms of his predecessor, Bob; it *was* necessary to know what was going on, without having to share that information with others.

There was no dust on the tracks now, for the subway was regularly used. He could not trace her visually. But when he put one ear to the metal he heard some faint brushing or knocking. Someone was walking along the track, headed for the hostel. Someone heavy, a bit clumsy . . . like a woman large with child.

He followed into the dark tunnel, running silently. Soon he could hear her directly, and he slowed to make sure he would not be prematurely detected. He wanted to catch her before she could do anything rash. Vara could be a difficult handful at the best of times. . . .

She was picking her way along as though afraid of the dark, making slow progress. One person, not two.

Why wasn't Sosa with her? Sosa was catlike in the dark, and she had other routes—but she would not leave her adopted daughter to stumble alone. Actually, Vara herself was a competent night marcher; pregnancy should not change that completely.

He came up behind her and spoke. "Go no farther."

"Oh!" It was a shriek of surprise, and something dropped.

The voice gave her away: Sola. She had been carrying her belongings in a bundle in her arms, together with what must be a fair amount of food and water. No wonder she lumbered!

"What are you doing here?" he demanded, perversely angry at her for not being Vara.

"I'm leaving!"

Obviously. "No one leaves Helicon. You know that better than anyone."

"Then kill me!" she cried, hysterically defiant. "I won't stay with *her!*"

176

Why did everyone associate him with killing, still? "Vara? But she needs you more than ever now—"

"Sosa!" The name was hissed.

Belatedly, he made the connection. If *he* resented Sosa's captivity of Vara's affection, how much more should Vara's natural mother resent being shunted aside at the very time she had expected to be closest to her daughter? He had been narrow to view Sosa's impact only as it applied to himself. He had overlooked the natural reactions of others—just as Bob had, before. Was he fated to make all the same mistakes, until the same end came?

"You have other responsibilities," he said, somewhat lamely. "You can't run away just because one thing isn't right." Yet he had been feeling an increasing temptation to do just that himself, for administration bored and annoyed him as it had when he was a leader in the nomad empire, and without Vara he had little to brighten his outlook. "Here in Helicon there are no mates, no parents, no children—only jobs to do."

"I know it!" she cried. "That's the trouble! I have no mate, no child!"

"Every man is your mate. You described the policy of Helicon yourself. Sharing."

She laughed bitterly. "I'm an old woman. Men don't share with me."

Neq saw that she had more than one grudge against the underworld. Had he been doing his own job properly, he would have been aware of this problem long since. He had to do something now, or admit he was less a leader than Bob had been. Yet it was impossible to restore to her the sexual attraction she had had a generation ago.

Deprived of both sexuality and motherhood in a situation where both were doubly important—no wonder Sola was miserable! "We need you in Helicon," he said. "I shall not let you go. There is no life for you outside."

"Sosa can do my job; talk to *her*."

"No! Sosa has a different temperament. She——" Then he had it. "She can't bear children!"

"Do you think *I* can?" Sola snapped. "I'm thirty-three years old!"

"You bore Vara! Then you lived with a castrate, and then a sterile man. When you tried with Var, he was sterile too. *They* could not make life; *you* could. And you can still! And Helicon must have that life! Children are our most important——"

"Childbirth would kill me at this age. I'm almost a grandmother." Yet he knew by her tone that she wanted to be convinced.

"Not with Dick the Surgeon attending. He made the Weaponless what he was——"

"Sterile!" she put in.

"That was an accident! Look what he did for these hands of mine! No one else could have restored me like that, and he didn't make *me* sterile! He can save life; he can save yours no matter how many babies you might bear, no matter how old. And if—it won't happen, but if—if you *do* die—*what difference does it make?* You'll die anyway in the wilderness!"

That bit of cruelty brought a perverse glimmer of hope to her face, but it passed. "No man will touch me," she said sullenly.

"*Every* man will touch you!" he cried. "This is Helicon, and I am master! I'll send——" he broke off, realizing this was the wrong approach. He was saying in effect that men had to be forced, and she would never go along with that.

"You see? *You* don't travel; you know what I mean."

He did know. Now he saw his duty. "When I first saw you, you were sixteen. You were beautiful—more lovely than any. I used to dream about you—lewd dreams."

"Did you?" She seemed genuinely flattered.

"You're older now—but so am I. You're bitter—and so am I. Yet we can do anything the youngsters can. I will

178

give you your baby—one no one can take away from you."

"You've done your duty already by my daughter," she said, the hint of a chuckle in her voice.

"That's over. The baby will not bear my name. I had to give her what I had taken from her. She will share hereafter—as will I. And you. You have beauty yet."

"Do I?" It was a little-girl query, plaintive.

There on the tracks he took her. And in the dark he found that he had spoken truly, and there was a lot of Vara in her, and it was better than he had expected.

CHAPTER TWENTY

It was just a faint whiff, but it brought a rash of strange feelings. Neq followed his nose.

There was a tiny crack in the wall he hadn't noticed before. From a distance it looked like an imperfection in the finish, but now he discovered that it was deep. Had Bob had a secret compartment in his office, along with all the rest?

He inserted the corner of a sheet of paper into it and probed. The paper disappeared—and now he had lost his weapons-production statistics for the past month! There was space in there, all right—and the odor was jetting out, a very small current of air.

He fetched a dagger and maneuvered it into the crack with his pincers. He pried. Something snapped, and a section of the wall swung in. There was a passage here—one he had missed, and might never have found, except for the little smell.

He peered in. It was dark, of course, and there was a warm draft. The odor was much stronger.

179

It was a man-hewn tunnel into the unexplored subterranean wilderness of Mt. Helicon. Anything at all could lie within, and the chances were more than even that it was deadly. This called for an armed party.

Neq shrugged and entered, alone. The stimulating breath of fragrance washed down along the corridor, lightening his step, and the stone and metal walls seemed to widen. This was Bob's escape route—and he had been right, a man needed such an exit from the tedium of leadership.

Vara had borne a fine boy and named him Vari. She had spent a reasonable period recovering and tending the baby, then begun sharing. Sosa spent considerable time with the baby also, and already it seemed as though Vari were hers. Three months after the first birth, Vara was pregnant again, and not by Neq.

Sola, too, conceived, and her joy transformed her. The two women became closer, not as mother and daughter but as sister-expectants, comparing notes and talking about plans for the Helicon nursery facilities and schooling of children. They were fine examples for the others, and the problems of the sharing system were diminishing.

Neq walked on, in a daze of memory despite the danger of exploring the unknown alone. He had a flashlight, for he never could anticipate when he might need light in Helicon, and he used it to pick out his path through the expanding passage. Now there was no metal, and the rock bore mosslike growths and was convoluted into treelike formations.

Jim the Gun had completed his initial renovation of the equipment and instituted a training program for operation and maintenance so that the work could carry on without him. "I'm not leaving," he said. "I like it here. Machines are my thing, and these are wondrous! But accidents happen, and I am aging."

As the machinery of Helicon moved toward capacity production—the capacity of the human attendants, not the machines—the exports to the crazies increased. The old trucks were renovated, for Helicon produced motors and tires and gasoline and gears, and the six trucks the crazies had been able to maintain became twenty, then fifty. Nomads had to be recruited as drivers and guards, being paid in food and good weapons and medicine. The trucks always traveled in convoys: one for the payload, another filled with warriors armed and spoiling for battle, the third carrying gasoline and replacement parts and food and similar staples. A new tribe formed: the trucker tribe, dedicated to this service. The existence and function of Helicon was no longer secret, of course, but the conditions of admittance remained stringent. The Truckers felt they had the best of it: Helicon provisions, a rambling nomad life. Many died in the actions against greedy outlaws, but this was the nomad way. Heroism.

The trail wandered between the overhanging trees, tunnel-like. Neq walked faster, eager to get where he was going.

He had wanted to have a crew lay down a telephone cable from Helicon to the main crazy outpost. But the expenditure in manpower would have been prohibitive, since they would have had either to raise the wire out of the casual reach of the outlaws, or bury it where it could not be found. There were mountains and rivers and badlands along the route. He had to settle for continuous radio contact, which would soon become television contact.

Dick the Surgeon started a hospital where nomads could receive medical attention and such drugs as required. But this posed another problem: either he had to leave Helicon, or nomads had to be admitted on a temporary basis. The old guidelines were inadequate. Neq dispensed with them. A portion of the underworld was blocked off from the rest, and a separate entrance opened. Dick began training those nomads who were interested in the potentials of medicine, though most of these were illiterate and ignorant. He had to devise simplified picture-codes for prescriptions: a circle with a jagged arrow through it representing a headache for aspirin; the outline of a tooth for novocain; a squiggle representing a germ for antibiotics. He made sure no dangerous drugs were available without his supervision, and the system worked well enough. The nomad trainees were not stupid; they merely had to learn.

But Neq declared that the children of Helicon should be literate. He set the example by attending classes himself, painstakingly mastering the words: MAN, ROOM, FOOD, HONOR. There was an enormous amount to be learned from the old books, and the new generation would not be able to improve on the past without understanding it. The present generation was too busy to practice reading, and Neq had to graduate after building a vocabulary of twenty words, but he knew that once Helicon was thoroughly established the priorities would change.

Yes, it was all going well. Neq was as successful in running Helicon as he had been in running his own tribe for the empire.

This region was familiar. The contour of the route, the type of forest—there was a dead-spoked giant pine he remembered. The memories were at once poignant and horrible, but he had to go on.

Vara's love had proved fickle. It was apparent that her affair with him had been the swing of the pendulum, compensation for her prior abuse of him. And his love for her—it had never compared to the sublime passion he had had for Neqa. He had succumbed to the lure of young flesh, thinking the experience more meaningful than it was. Vara had merely started sharing early, that Helicon might be repopulated.

Neqa: there was the meaning of it all. He had done what he had done to bring back the world that sponsored her kind—but he had not brought *her* back. This was where Yod's barricade had been set across the trail, balking their truck. Yod's tribe was gone now, of course, and even the staring skulls on poles were gone. Vengeance. . . .

It was time to make camp, for he had come far. Neq bared his sword to cut down saplings for a temporary lean-to. The gleaming steel reminded him: had he demonstrated just a bit of his sworder-skill and agreed to join Yod's outlaw tribe, he could have saved his hands and Neqa's life. Were he in the same situation today, he would do it. She would have had to share—but would that have been so very different from Vara's sharing at Helicon, after bearing the child of her husband's murderer? Would Neqa have been unworthy of his love after bearing Yod's child? She could have borne fifty children by other men, if that were the price of preserving her life! With greater circumspection he could have bided his time and eventually assumed the mastery of the tribe and recovered his woman. He had acted impetuously—and paid a grievous price.

Dusk—and someone was coming!

Neq's blade lifted, ready. He did not wish to kill—but this place was in its way sacred to him, and the man who abused his privacy would be in trouble.

In the gloom of evening beneath the dense forest, Neq paced the man more by sound than sight. The tread was light yet not furtive.

Now he saw the figure: small, very small, with no visible weapon.

"Neq!"

By the voice he knew her: Sosa.

"What are you doing here?" he demanded, knowing she had followed him all the way from the mountain: several days swift march. Did she seek to bring him back as he had brought Sola back?

"I smelled the flowers," she said. "I tend them now, and I thought it was a leak, but it wasn't. So I traced it to your office . . . I'm almost immune, after these months with the vine. But you—"

Neq stepped toward her, lifting the sword. But even in

183

the worst of his vengeance he had not attacked women.

"I was afraid of that," she murmured. "I'll have to watch you, until I can locate the plants and shut them off."

She walked by him, passing quite close, and he was aware of her athletic surprisingly attractive body. Women didn't *have* to fade as they aged! Bemused, he followed her, not certain what she intended or what he desired.

Then he recognized her destination. "Stay clear of that grave!" he cried.

"Grave? That's your real wound, isn't it?" she said. "Ah, I think this is it. The passage is blocked, but there's an updraft—"

She began to scrape away the leaves and twigs that covered the site of Neqa's grave, exposing the rich earth beneath. "This is garbage!" she exclaimed.

Neq raised the sword again. "Stop, or surely you must die!"

"I'm doing this for you," she said, continuing. "The draft is bringing the fumes straight out. The flowers must be just beyond this refuse."

"I would not slay a woman," Neq said, his blade poised above her body. "But if I must—"

"In a moment I'll have it," she said. "Meanwhile, please don't threaten me with that thing. If you knew how many times I have been widowed, you would see that your sorrow is hardly unique. I don't care what you think you see; I have a job to do here."

He saw that she would not stop. But he could not allow Neqa's bones to be defiled.

He spread his arms so that the sword would not strike her and moved forward, shoving her aside with his body. His own torso would guard the sacred earth!

But Sosa's dirt-caked hands came up, striking him across the neck so that he choked. She got her little shoulder under him and somehow threw him back.

"Please stay clear," she said quietly. "There may be danger, and I have to get this junk out."

Now he remembered what Vara had said about this woman. She was skilled, circle-skilled, with her bare hands! She had taught the Weaponless his art. It was folly to attempt to wrestle with her.

Numbly, he watched the hole deepen. It was not mere bones she was searching out. He had no idea whether anything at all remained of Neqa after all these years. It was the associations of Neqa—the manner she had died, the way he had acted then. The nightmare portion of his nomad dream, that he had tried to put aside. Rape, murder, anguish, vengeance, futility. . . .

She struck solidity. Horrified, Neq shone the light as she reached down, grasped, and hauled up—

A hooflike foot.

Appalled, Neq stumbled back. This was the cairn of Var the Stick—the other nightmare!

The foot stirred, the gross blunted toes twitching. Earth showered off as the hairy leg kicked out of the ground.

"Oh-oh," Sosa said. "I didn't expect *this*!" She scrambled away from the hole.

An arm came up, levering against the surface. The body heaved. The corpse sat up.

The shock of it sobered Neq momentarily, and he realized that he was under the influence of the narcotic vine-flowers, as Sosa had tried to tell him. They must have seeded here, for the fumes were actually pollen, and there had been some leakages. If there were earth here, and moisture, and occasional light, the vines could have sprouted and bloomed.

The corpse was neither Neqa nor Var, but some living thing climbing out of the partially stopped passage. Something manlike—but *what*? Already his vision was becoming distorted again, for the fumes were heavy in this semi-confined space.

Neq tapped on the glockenspiel with his pincers, but

185

could not think of a suitable song for the occasion.

"I thought you were dead!" Sosa cried at the shape.

A grotesquely formless head swiveled to cover her. "Hel-Helicon dead!" it growled.

"Helicon *lives!*" Neq cried, discovering suddenly loyalty after his recent, drug-strengthened doubts. He brought up his sword—and hesitated, knowing that so long as he saw it as a sword, the narcotic was ruling his mind. "Stop those flowers!" he cried at Sosa. "Use my flashlight—"

She came immediately and took it from him. She could use it far more effectively than he could with the pincers. She flashed it into the hole, searching for the vines that had to be near.

Neq faced the creature. "Who are you?" he demanded.

"Dead!" the thing repeated. It stood near the hole, as tall as a man, but with a scarred, hairless head.

"It's Bob," Sosa said. "Master of Helicon."

The former master! So he *had* escaped Sol's vengeance!

"I am master now," Neq said. "You and I must settle."

"Get out of here, Neq!" Sosa cried. "He's a *real* killer, and you're under the influence of the—"

"This way," Bob said. His voice was barely intelligible, as though it had not been used for years.

"Don't go there!" Sosa cried. "He's mad!"

The men ignored her. Bob descended into the grave and Neq followed, feeling with his pincers to locate the perimeters. He crawled along on elbows and knees, keeping his sword clear of the rubble. Sosa did not follow.

They emerged into a palatial cavern whose floor angled down into a steaming river: the Helicon water supply. It was hot here, and there was light: electric light from bulbs set in the ceiling.

"You've had power here—the whole time?"

"Certainly." Bob's voice was clearer now that he was in his own territory, and the flower fragrance was fading. "I prepared this refuge well, in case of need. There's a vent to the summit of the mountain, with a ladder and escape hatch."

"Why did you stay here, then?"

"It's cold up there." That was an understatement. The top of the mountain was always covered with snow, and death lurked in the form of countless cliffs and crevasses and avalanches. Mighty storms spun off the glaciers, feeding the melt-rivers of the snowline whose waters plunged into these atomically heated interior caverns. It would take a desperate man indeed to leave comfort like this to endure that.

"You are alone?" It was hard to believe that any man could endure seven years in complete isolation.

"Of course not. I have a most obliging and disciplined tribe. Come—you must see. I have no envy of your position." He showed the way along the river to a series of offshoot caverns.

There were animals here-mutant badlands creatures of diverse shapes and sizes. Some slunk away as the men approached, but others seemed to be tame. "These?" Neq asked.

"This is part of it. These are workers and gatherers—illiterate, of course. They do an excellent job of tending and harvesting the hydroponics, but they aren't very intelligent."

Neq saw that the ratlike individuals were nipping bits of fungus from crevices and carrying them away. "Hydroponics," he agreed.

"You really must meet my wife," Bob said expansively. "One thing about the life of the Helicon master: no woman to yourself."

"I know." So one of the women had come there too!

"That forced objectivity, when there are constant decisions of life and death, and no personal life—it isn't Helicon you've inherited, it's Hell."

Neq had learned about Hell through his songs. The parallel seemed apt enough. "I saw your traces in the dining room. I wondered who had visited."

"Traces? Not mine. I blocked up the passage with refuse and never used it, until you started burrowing from the other side just now. I had to investigate that commotion, of course."

Refuse—and the vine-flower spores had rooted there, downwind from Bob's caverns but upwind from Helicon. They had grown and blossomed, betraying the secret. Sosa had not been excavating Neqa's grave or Var's cairn, but Bob's refuge.

"Why did you try to kill the child Soli?" Neq asked as though it were a matter of mere curiosity. Once he had a clear answer coinciding with what he already knew of the matter, he could consider his action. This time he would make no precipitous mistake!

"I never tried to kill her. I tried to save Helicon."

"You failed."

"The failure was not mine. I knew that no nomad would kill either a woman or a child, especially one as fetching as little Soli. I knew that the barbarian warrior, meeting her in the secrecy of the mesa, would either allow her the victory or hide her unharmed and claim the victory himself. In either case, Helicon was safe."

Bob, sealed in these caverns, could not have known the story of Var and Soli. He had calculated correctly— except for the human factor within Helicon. "Safe?"

"If she had the victory, the nomads were honor-bound to lift the siege. If she were announced dead, my revelation of her identity would neutralize the nomad leader and have the same effect. Sos knew how to put pressure on the mountain; he was a superb military tactician, and he had studied our defenses from inside. He might have won—but no other nomad would have had either the motive or the ability."

Somehow it made sense—except that it had failed. "Why didn't you tell the others your strategy?"

"A leader never tips his hand in advance. Surely you know that. I had to make it work, then explain it or not, as seemed best. Premature information could have been disastrous."

Neq wondered how well his song and flower gambit

would have worked, had the group known what he was doing before he assumed the leadership. He knew the answer. Bob was right. Except: "But Sol fired Helicon!"

Bob glanced at him. "That barbarian? He lacked the wit. *I* fired Helicon."

Amazed, Neq said nothing.

"Somehow the fool librarian got hold of some of the information and the word spread before I was ready to explain. Sol charged toward my office intending to attack me personally, and I saw in the monitors that the others actually sided with the fool. I have no tolerance for such short-sightedness. So I pushed the DESTRUCT button on my desk and came here. I never cared to return; it would have been messy."

"Vengeance?" Neq asked softly, muscles taut.

"There is no profit in vengeance; you'll learn that one day," Bob said condescendingly. "It was merely practicality. When discipline deteriorates, the organization is defunct. It is kinder to terminate it outright."

"But the entire nomad society collapsed!"

Bob shrugged. "One must accept the consequence of one's mistakes."

It was plausible. Bob had known what he was doing. When others had tried to interfere, he had acted most effectively to suppress the mutiny. This was true leadership. Had Bob been in Neq's situation seven years ago, he would have arranged to kill Yod before Neqa ever was threatened. Neq knew that next to this man he was an innocent; he lacked the fortitude to do what was necessary. Neq had blundered through life, either prevailing extemporaneously or suffering harshly.

They came to another large cavern. "Ah, here she is," Bob said. "A fine, loyal woman who embodies the very principles of obedience and trust and discretion I require. Had the functionaries of Helicon only been similar . . ."

A shaggy, bearlike creature with aquatic flipper-feet shuffled up: another fringe mutant. "Pleased to meet you, Boba," Neq said.

189

"Not Boba—that's decadent nomad nomenclature," Bob corrected him. "*Mrs.* Bob."

Neq nodded gravely. "Now I understand."

They met him the other side of the grave-dump. "What happened?" Jim demanded. "Did you kill him?"

"Of course not," Neq said, walking briskly on. "There is no profit in vengeance."

"But Bob was responsible for all the—" Sosa began.

"He has accepted the consequence of his mistake," Neq said. "As have I. Seal off the passage, and don't worry about the vines there; they make no difference." The fragrance was strong here, and he wanted to get out of it before his judgment was distorted again.

"Almost forgot," Jim said. "Someone's been trying to reach us on the radio—not the crazies. I had it switched to your office, but—"

In moments Neq was there. The voice emerging from the speaker was foreign. He strode out of the tunnel and touched his broadcast button. "Speak English!" he snapped. "This is Helicon." Too bad the narcotic didn't make all things intelligible!

After a brief delay another voice came through, accented. "This is the Andes station. We have been trying to reach you. There has been no contact for seven years—"

"Merely an interruption," Neq said.

"But we sent an envoy by helicopter two years ago, and he reported that your premises were deserted—"

So that was the mysterious visitor! "There has been a change in personnel. We regret that our former leader, Robert, has had to retire. I am Neq. You may deal with me henceforth."

The voice sounded worried. "We dealt many years with Robert. How did he die?"

"Please, Andes!" Neq said, affecting shock. "Helicon is civilized! Bob left his position in order to devote his full energies to his wife—a charming creature. Send your representative again and we'll introduce him."

There was a pause. Then: "That will not be necessary. Are you in normal operation again? Do you need assistance?"

"How is your supply of young women?" Neq asked.

"How is your supply of electronic equipment?"

Neq smiled. He had a job to do, and suddenly he liked it.

A SELECTED LIST OF SCIENCE FICTION FOR YOUR READING PLEASURE